KICKOFF!

KICKOFF!

Tiki and Ronde Barber
with Paul Mantell

SCHOLASTIC INC.
New York Toronto London Auckland Sydney
Mexico City New Delhi Hong Kong Buenos Aires

For AJ and Chason—T. B.

For my three Roses—R. B.

To my wife and partner, Avery,
and my sons, Clay and Matt,
for all their love and support—P. M.

ACKNOWLEDGMENTS
The authors and publisher gratefully acknowledge Mark
Lepselter for his help in making this book.

ISBN-13: 978-0-545-09668-3
ISBN-10: 0-545-09668-5

12 11 10 9 8 7 6 5 4 3 2   8 9 10 11 12 13/0

Printed in the U.S.A.   23

First Scholastic printing, September 2008

Book design by Kristin Smith
The text for this book is set in Melior.

CHAPTER ONE

THE END OF SUMMER

"HUT! HUT! GO LONG, TIKI!"

Ronde Barber gripped the football with both hands. He dropped back three steps—just like Joe Theismann of the Redskins, his favorite pro quarterback. Ronde's fingers found the ball's laces, and he cocked his arm back to make the pass.

His identical twin, Tiki, sprinted down the sideline. Fast as lightning, Tiki blew right by the defender—their best friend, Paco, who was big and strong, but not fast. No one was as fast as Tiki, it seemed.

Ronde threw the ball—a perfect spiral!

But it landed ten feet short.

"Oh, man!" Their teammate Jason threw both hands up in frustration. "Why can't *I* be the quarterback, like always? Your hands are too small to get a good grip on the ball."

"They are not!" Ronde grabbed the football from Paco, who'd brought it back to the line of scrimmage— right in the middle of Mews Hill Drive—and spread his fingers over the laces. "See?"

"Whatever," Jason said, frowning. "I'm still a better quarterback than you."

1

Ronde had to admit it was true. Last spring their team, the Vikings, had won the Peewee League championship. And even though everyone on the team had a chance to play lots of different positions, Jason had done most of the quarterbacking.

All three boys were still proud of that championship— in fact, they were all wearing their bright purple Vikings jerseys today.

Jason had had his growth spurt when he was twelve. Now, at thirteen, he was tall and skinny, with big hands that could grip a football like it was nothing. He could throw a perfect spiral thirty, even forty yards.

Ronde and Tiki were still small for twelve. But they'd get bigger sooner or later—at least, Ronde sure hoped so. They were identical twins, but their friends could tell them apart. Tiki was quieter and liked history. Ronde's favorite subject was math. But one thing was for sure— they both loved football. They lived for it.

"Car!" Adam yelled, and they all retreated to the curb until it passed by.

They didn't have to dodge cars too often. This block of Mews Hill Drive was an unpaved dead end, petering out into the driveway of a large empty lot. Once there had been an old mill there, but now it was just a crumbling chimney, surrounded by acres of weeds. Lately, though, there had been more traffic. People in suits came by every day to look at the empty lot.

Whenever a car did come along, Adam was always the first to spot it. A tall kid with bad posture and thick glasses, he wasn't strong, or fast, or much of an athlete. His one claim to fame was that he could kick the ball a mile.

"Okay, third down," Paco said, panting. "Let's get this over with."

"Why? You tired?" Tiki teased.

"Yeah, I'm tired—I'm tired of chasing after you. How come you're not out of breath?"

Tiki shrugged. "Beats me. I like running."

"Oh, man," Paco said. "Give it a rest."

"What's the matter?" Tiki asked, laughing. "You not having fun?"

"Forty-nine to seven is *not fun*," Paco said.

"Not when you're the seven."

"He's right," Adam said. "It's no fair when you and Ronde are on the same team."

"Hey, man," Ronde said, "We're all gonna be on the same team from now on. Starting next week, we'll be part of the Hidden Valley Eagles. Next thing you know, it'll be high school, then college, and right on up to the Redskins, and the Super Bowl. Right, Tiki?"

"No, man, not the Redskins—the Bears!" Tiki corrected him. "Walter Payton's the man!"

Tiki, Ronde, and Jason huddled up, while Chris, Paco, and Adam waited at the line of scrimmage.

"Okay," Ronde whispered to his teammates. "I'll fake a

3

handoff to Jason. Tiki, fake a screen, then go long again."

"I just went long," Tiki said. "And you couldn't reach me!"

"Let me be quarterback this play, Ronde," Jason pleaded.

"Give it up, dude," Ronde said. "*I'm* the quarterback today. We drew for it, remember?"

"Just don't go long again, okay?" Jason begged.

"All right, all right," Ronde said, frowning. "Fake to you, then handoff to Tiki."

They lined up at scrimmage. And right on cue, Chris started doing his sportscasting routine. True, they were only playing three-on-three touch football on an unpaved dead-end street—but Chris made it sound much bigger and more important.

"And the Bears line up. The quarterback takes the snap, hands off to—no, wait, it's a fake! And now he gives it to Payton! Payton cuts through the line! Uh-oh, Lawrence Taylor's after him—but Payton somehow gets away! He's at the twenty, the ten—*touchdown!* Touchdown, Bears! Walter Payton does it again! *Yaaaay!*"

The way he got excited, you'd have thought Chris was on Tiki's team instead of Paco's. "And it's fifty-six to seven, Bears!"

"Oh, man, can we call this game on the mercy rule?" Paco begged. "Let's choose up new teams."

"Nah, it's almost dinnertime," Chris said. "My mom wants me home early to eat, because we're going out shopping tonight for school supplies."

"Ugh. Now you're *really* depressing me," Paco said. "Don't remind me about school—it's still summer."

"You mean it's still summer till tomorrow," Tiki said. "Hey, Paco, how come you hate school so much?"

"I don't hate it. I just like summer better. . . ."

Ronde could tell there was more to it than that. Paco looked . . . well, almost *scared* to go to junior high.

"Well, hey," Ronde said, "we're all gonna be on the Hidden Valley Eagles. That'll be cool, right?"

"That'll be *awesome*," Tiki agreed, and the kids all slapped one another five.

As they headed back to their houses for dinner, Ronde put his arm around his brother's shoulders. "You and me, Tiki—we're gonna be the stars of the team."

Tiki grinned. "I can't wait, can you?"

"Nope. I wonder how soon tryouts are gonna be. . . ."

The sun was setting. The giant neon star at the top of Mill Mountain flickered on. Soon it would light up the night over Roanoke, Virginia.

Ronde wondered if he and Tiki would someday be stars, too . . . stars in the NFL.

"Hey, you guys—wait up!" It was Paco, jogging after them, breathing hard, his face red and sweaty.

"So what was that about before, Paco?" Ronde asked.

"What was *what* about?"

"You're so down on going back to school, man." Tiki said. "Even if you want it to, summer can't last forever.

5

And, hey, you get As and Bs in everything, like we do."

"Everything except *math*," Paco corrected him. "Besides, my brother James says the work in junior high is mad hard."

Tiki laughed. "Dude, you *like* homework, remember? You always do it right after school, before you play football or anything."

"I just do it that way to get it over with," Paco said. "Besides, you guys do it right after school too."

"We have to," Ronde said. "Our mom makes us."

"Yeah, it's not 'cause we *want* to." Tiki shook his head. "I could never think like you, Paco. You are truly bizarre."

Ronde gave Paco a playful shove. "Come on, dude, what are you scared of, anyway? It's gonna be fun."

"That's what you think," Paco said.

Tiki said, "I think going from class to class is gonna be awesome. Just think, if you don't like your teacher, just wait an hour and you're with a different one! And anyhow, after seven years I'm ready for a new school."

"It's not that," Paco said, stopping and looking down at the ground. "It's . . . oh, never mind."

"Tell us, dude," Tiki said, putting an arm around him. "Hey, we're best buds, right? You can tell us anything."

Paco sighed heavily. "All right. But don't go freaking out when I tell you."

He looked first at Tiki, then at Ronde. "My brother James? You know, he's starting high school, but he went to

Hidden Valley till last year. And he told me they have this day . . . it's supposed to be the second day of school—that's this Thursday. It's called 'Beat the Seventh Graders Day.' And on that day, guess what happens? All the ninth graders hunt down the new kids and *pound them*."

"*WHAT?*" both Barber boys said at once.

"That's just crazy talk," Tiki said, snorting.

"Yeah. James is just goofing on you," Ronde agreed.

He and Tiki nodded at one another, but Ronde could tell that Tiki was just a little scared.

In fact Ronde had to admit he was a little worried himself—even though it was probably all just a load of baloney.

"James said, the year he was a seventh grader, two kids wound up in the hospital, and three got black eyes and bloody noses."

"Did *he* get one?" Tiki asked.

"*James*? No, man!" Paco said. "You know my brother— he's like six foot three, two-twenty. He was big back then, too—and they don't pick on the big kids."

"Then what are *you* worried about?" Ronde asked.

"Man, I'm not *that* big," Paco said. "You should see some of those kids in junior high. The guys on the football team? If they ever tackle you, it'll break your bones!"

They'd reached Paco's corner. "I'll see you dudes at school tomorrow, huh?" he said. "But maybe you'd better both play hooky on Thursday—*you know why*."

7

The Barber boys ran the whole rest of the way up Mews Hill Drive to their home, tossing the football back and forth between them. They pretended they were on the field, dodging invisible defenders.

It kept them from thinking about "Beat the Seventh Graders Day."

Ronde could smell his mom's cooking as soon as they reached their corner.

"Mmmm . . . macaroni and cheese!" Tiki said, grinning.

Tiki and Ronde's mom was a great cook. She was lots of fun, too—even though she had to work long hours at the local Girl Scout council office, where she was a secretary. On top of it all, she could throw a mean football. But most important, Ronde and Tiki knew they could always count on her to be there for them.

Smelling their favorite dish, they stopped tossing the ball and flat-out raced the rest of the way home. They banged the screen door open so hard it sounded like an explosion.

"Whoa!" their mother yelled, so surprised that she dropped her spatula. "You boys need to slow down! You could scare somebody to death."

"Sorry, Ma," Tiki said.

"Sorry," said Ronde, retrieving the spatula for her.

"Now please take off those muddy shoes and get cleaned up for dinner," she said. "We're having mac and cheese."

"Yes, ma'am!" said the boys, and raced each other to the bathroom sink, bumping, blocking, and laughing all the way.

• • •

After dinner, the boys cleared the table and helped their mom do the dishes. Only when everything was cleaned up did she hand each of them an envelope. "It's your program cards from school," she said.

Ronde and Tiki had been waiting for this moment for weeks. They couldn't wait to see which classes they had— and most important, who was in each class with them.

"I've got math first period," Tiki moaned. "At seven thirty in the morning!"

"What's wrong with that?" their mom asked.

"I'm not even awake that early, and everyone says that math in junior high is hard!"

"Well, you were bound to have *some* class first period," their mom said, patting him on the shoulder. "It might as well be math."

"Hey," Ronde said, comparing his own program card to his brother's. "We don't have any classes together!"

"What?" Tiki gasped, looking for himself. "Not one single class? Hey, Ma, can we get these changed?"

"Yeah, we've gotta get things switched around!" Ronde agreed. "They must have made a mistake!"

Their mom folded her arms in front of her and frowned. "There's no mistake. You boys have got to learn how to get by on your own. All your lives you've been a pair, and that's a beautiful thing. But you're starting to

9

grow up now, and you've got to learn what it's going to be like when you're grown-ups."

"Ma," Ronde said, a choking feeling in his throat, "did you *ask* for it to be this way?"

Their mom's face softened. "I won't lie to you boys. Yes, I did ask that you be in separate classes. I want you to be close all your lives, but I think it's better if you start spending time on your own with other kids. Stand up for yourselves, and make new friends to go with the old."

"Aw, Ma," Ronde complained, "we've already got plenty of friends!"

"I know it—but I don't want them to think of you boys as half of something. Once you're out on your own a little, you'll see what I mean."

"Can't we have just *one* class together?" Tiki begged.

"You can see each other every day at lunch," she pointed out. "And of course, there are your after-school activities, like the football team. . . ."

That was true, Ronde thought. But it didn't make up for all the hours and hours he'd be sitting in school alone, without his brother.

He looked over at Tiki, and Tiki stared back at him.

True identical twins, at certain moments, they thought exactly the same things. This was one of those moments.

Only an hour ago, they'd been totally excited about to going to Hidden Valley Junior High. Now, they both wished the day would never come.

CHAPTER TWO

SCHOOL DAZE

AS SHE DID EVERY YEAR ON THE FIRST MORNING of school, the twins' mom fixed each boy a special breakfast, including some of their all-time favorites. For Ronde, it was bacon and eggs with one pancake and OJ. For Tiki, three pancakes, ham, and a glass of milk. Their mom also made sure their book bags held everything the twins needed—pens, pencils, rulers, calculators, notebooks, and lunch money.

One thing was different this year, though—Ronde and Tiki could choose their own clothes. Mrs. Barber wanted to make sure that they were as different as could be, so the other kids—the ones they'd be meeting for the first time—could tell them apart. So they made sure they never matched.

When she hugged and kissed them on the cheek and sent them off to the bus, the hugs were extra tight, and there was an extra kiss or two for each boy, as if to say, *This is a big day for you both. Good luck.*

As the boys rode off to school, they were unusually silent. Neither Tiki nor Ronde were big talkers anyway, but today they were even quieter than usual. Instead of talking, each boy was deep in his own thoughts.

Tiki wondered what it would be like, being in class without his twin. He was used to new kids staring at them because they looked so alike. Would they still stare at him, now that he was alone?

And what would it be like having so many different teachers? Would they each give a ton of homework, not realizing that all the other teachers were doing the same thing?

Why did their mom have to insist that they not have even one single class together? Tiki was so upset about it, he felt like crying—but he couldn't let himself—no way. He didn't want anyone—least of all Ronde—knowing how he was feeling right then. Afraid.

Hidden Valley Junior High School was a boxy, gigantic building—much bigger than their elementary school. Tiki knew that was because kids from other elementaries went there, too. He wondered if he'd know *anybody* in his classes.

"Well, I guess this is it," he said as they climbed the front steps and the early bell sounded. "See you at lunch?"

"I guess," Ronde said. His voice sounded strange to Tiki—thicker than usual, somehow. Tiki wondered if Ronde was trying to hide his feelings too.

Probably, he figured. After all, they were identical twins, and that meant they often thought—and felt—the same way about things.

It was scary to think that maybe that would soon be ending too, now that they weren't going to be together all the time.

"Okay. Bye," he said, giving Ronde a quick nod and going inside.

Tiki fished out his program card and checked it one more time. "Math—room 208," he read. He found a staircase and started up to the second floor, lost in a sea of unfamiliar faces.

Wait—there was that kid Kevin, who was in his class way back in second grade! Tiki wondered whether he should wave, or say hello. He decided not to risk it— Kevin might not even remember him after all this time. He might think Tiki was weird for saying hi, considering they barely knew each other.

The rest of the way up the stairs, Tiki concentrated on the floor. So many feet! All those different kinds of shoes . . . Were his cool enough? He'd figured he couldn't go wrong with sneakers, but then, you never knew.

He bumped into the girl in front of him when she stopped at the door to the second floor. "Sorry," he said, glancing up at her.

She clicked her tongue, rolled her eyes, and said, "Watch where you're going, stupid."

Tiki felt like a complete idiot! Why did he have to bump into that girl? And why did she have to be so mean about it? Was everybody in this school going to be as mean as her?

13

He felt like running right back down the stairs and outside, back into the beautiful September morning. But he knew he couldn't.

He found room 208, and headed straight for the back of the classroom, where he zoned in on the last available empty seat. Tiki was determined to sit in the back of the class, where he could hide from the teacher's gaze whenever he didn't know the answer to a question. He usually knew—but just hated to be wrong.

But before he could reach the seat, another boy bumped him out of the way and plunked himself down in it!

Tiki turned around and checked out the rest of the seats. He quickly grabbed one in the third row—as far from the teacher's desk as he could get. Tiki promised himself that when this class was over, he'd run like the wind to get to his next classroom, so he'd have plenty of time to find a seat in the back row.

His math teacher, Mr. Vaughn, was incredibly boring. He spoke in a monotone, and never smiled.

And the math was *hard*! Whenever Mr. Vaughn talked about algebra, Tiki got so confused it felt like his eyes were crossing.

Pretty soon, Tiki found himself feeling sleepy. He wasn't used to getting up so early in the morning—he and Ronde had set their alarm for six thirty to get to school by seven thirty—and he hadn't slept well besides, what with all those nightmares about school. Tiki had to keep stopping himself from nodding off, to avoid making a fool of himself.

Maybe it was the big breakfast Mom made us, he thought. Big meals always had a way of making him sleepy. Or maybe it was just that Mr. Vaughn was *so boring!*

Tiki couldn't wait for the bell to ring. When it finally did, he took off at full speed, running down the hallway and dodging the other kids in his way. He held his book bag like a football, and pretended he was the great Walter Payton, dodging defenders as he raced for the end zone.

"Hey! Watch it!" yelled one kid after Tiki passed him by, nearly knocking him into the wall.

"Slow down there!" called a teacher who was acting as hall monitor. Tiki did, but only for a minute.

He got to history class just in time to grab a seat in the back row, all the way in the corner. Then he took a minute to catch his breath as the other seats began to fill up.

The front rows were taken up by the brainy kids—most of them girls—who always raised their hands for every question. Tiki didn't care. It seemed to him that they were less interested in learning new things than they were in showing off what they already knew.

Tiki usually knew the right answers, no matter what the class. But he almost never raised his hand. He didn't want to risk being wrong. If you were wrong, everybody thought you were stupid. Even if they didn't laugh in class, they would behind your back.

History class wound up being not too bad—it was his favorite subject, after all, and the teacher was a nice lady, Ms. Walker, who didn't give them any homework because it was the first day of school. But Tiki could tell that once things got going, she'd be giving out plenty of work.

As soon as the bell rang, he did another magnificent job of open-field running to get to science class, and grabbed another prized seat in the back row. The class slowly filled with kids—hey, there was Adam! Tiki's mood started to brighten. He'd always liked science— and whoever the teacher was, he or she had to be better than Mr. Vaughn!

The late bell rang, and a second later, the teacher walked in. He had a beard that was starting to go gray, and a shock of dark hair on top of his head that went in all directions. "Hello, everyone," he said. "My name is Sam Wheeler, but you can call me . . . Mr. Wheeler."

The kids laughed, and Tiki started to relax. Mr. Wheeler had a sense of humor, and that could only be good.

"First, I want everyone to stand up," Mr. Wheeler said. When the kids were all standing, he continued, "Okay, everyone in the two back rows, switch seats with the two front rows."

A loud groan went up from all the kids in the rows he'd mentioned. "I've found that it's best to get the slackers up front right away," said Mr. Wheeler. "That way, they can't get away with sleeping through *class*! And you kids in the front, take a break, will you? I already know you know the answers."

Whoa, thought Tiki, as he shuffled miserably up to the front row. *This guy must be some kind of mind reader.*

Mr. Wheeler started talking about the topics they'd be covering that year in Science. But the whole time he was talking, he kept scanning the class. He had the face of a hawk, or an eagle—yeah, that was it, Tiki thought. An eagle—that nose, those eyes . . . Mr. Wheeler could have been the school mascot!

His eyes drilled right into you. Tiki was terrified of those eyes—especially after Mr. Wheeler spotted Adam whispering to the kid next to him. Mr. Wheeler crumpled a piece of paper into a hard little ball, raised his right hand, and fired!

The paper ball hit Adam right between the shoulders. "Hey! Pay attention!" Mr. Wheeler said.

Adam turned around, his face beet red. The whole class laughed their heads off. It wasn't like anyone thought it was so funny, Tiki figured—they were just relieved it wasn't *them*.

"I'm not here for my health," said Mr. Wheeler, scanning the class again with those eagle eyes. "I'm here for *you*—so don't disrespect me." Then he went back to teaching.

The day's lesson was about the planets of the solar system. Tiki had always dreamed of being an astronaut, and normally, he would have been very interested. But for some reason—and in spite of his fear of Mr. Wheeler—Tiki soon found himself fighting the urge to sleep.

He checked his watch—it was only ten thirty, but he'd already been in school for three whole hours! More important, he'd been up since six thirty in the morning.

Waves of exhaustion washed over him, and he had to keep willing himself to keep his eyes open. He wondered if Ronde was going through the same thing. He wondered what football tryouts would be like that afternoon. He wondered . . .

Suddenly he felt something hard hit him on the head!

Tiki sprang to attention. The whole class was looking at him, laughing! He reached up and felt the top of his head, then looked on top of his desk. There was a crumpled-up ball of paper on it.

Oh, no!

"Did I say to pay attention, or didn't I?" Mr. Wheeler asked Tiki.

"Yes," Tiki murmured.

"What? I can't hear you!"

"Yes, *sir!*" More nervous laughter from the class, glad it wasn't them.

"I won't tolerate disrespect. Get it through your heads right *now*, people. All right; let's get on with—"

Mercifully, the bell rang, and it was time for lunch. Not

a moment too soon, either. Tiki rushed out of the room and ran for the cafeteria as if his life depended on it.

This was turning out to be the worst day of his whole entire life.

Ronde was in a panic. Here he was in his last class before lunch, math—always his best subject—and he had no idea what the teacher was talking about!

He thought back to sixth grade, when Miss Johnson had first introduced them to algebra. He hadn't really understood it. Why hadn't he raised his hand back then to ask her to explain?

Ronde knew why he hadn't—because everyone would have laughed at him. But if only he'd taken that chance in sixth grade, he wouldn't have been so lost now!

If only somebody else would raise their hand and ask Ms. Black to go over it again! But nobody did. And no way was Ronde going to raise *his* hand and admit he had no clue!

He was sure all the other kids already knew about algebra. He could tell, by the questions the brainy kids in the front row asked. He was sitting up front too—right in the middle of them—but keeping his hand firmly down.

The first day of school hadn't been so bad until now. He'd gotten through almost the whole morning without any awful stuff happening, and lunch was coming up. If he could just get through the next ten minutes without messing up, he could relax for almost a whole hour. He'd see Tiki; they'd sit together and compare notes, and everything would feel normal again.

And then, after a few more classes . . . football tryouts!

Ronde couldn't wait. He was so excited about it, he'd almost forgotten about Beat the Seventh Graders Day.

Almost.

"Hello? Earth to Ronde?"

It was Ms. Black, calling his name!

Ronde came to instant attention. "Um, could you repeat the question?"

"What? For the *fourth* time?"

The whole class exploded into laughter. Ronde felt like sliding down under his desk, and staying there forever.

Why hadn't he been paying attention? Why hadn't he raised his hand once, just to show her he was listening? Sure, he might have given the wrong answer, but *any* answer would have been better than none at all!

Now he looked like a complete idiot.

"Very well—what is the square root of one hundred forty-four?" Ms. Black asked.

"Um . . ." Ronde tried to remember how to do square roots. He *used* to know. But it had been a long summer, and now he couldn't recall. "Three?" he guessed.

The teacher made a "tsk" sound with her tongue. "Somebody else. Yes, Norman?"

Norman had been holding his hand up the whole

time, going "Ooo! Ooo!" Now he smirked at Ronde and said, "Twelve."

"That's right," Ms. Black said. "Very good, Norman. Now, Ronde, I want you to review pages 133 to 135 in your math book tonight. In fact, *all* of you had better review it—there'll be a quiz on it later this week."

A groan went up from the class. "Thanks a lot, Ronde," said the kid next to him. "Thanks a billion jillion."

Ronde headed to lunch feeling totally bummed. But before he entered the cafeteria, he took a deep breath, and tried to act like everything was normal. Just in case Tiki'd had a great morning, Ronde didn't want to look like a loser by telling his brother how badly things had gone.

He spotted Tiki, standing in the lunch line. "Hey, what's up?" Ronde greeted him.

"Hey," Tiki said. "How's it going?"

"Great. Great," Ronde said. "You?"

"Awesome."

"Yeah?"

"Yeah. You?"

"Fantastic."

"Great."

"Yeah. Me too."

By this time, a bunch of other kids had gathered around the brothers. "Hey, check this out!" said a boy Ronde recognized from English class—a real pain by the name of Kelvin. "I'm seein' double!"

"Me too!" said another boy, obviously a friend of Kelvin's. "It's the attack of the clones!"

"Yaaaa!!" The two boys started pretending to freak out. Everyone around them laughed, while Tiki and Ronde just stood there, taking it.

"Help! They're multiplying! Aaaahh!!"

Tiki and Ronde picked out their food, paid for it, and headed for a table over in the corner—as far away from Kelvin and his obnoxious buddies as they could get.

"This food looks like crud," Tiki said, checking out his plate. "What'd you get?"

"Welsh Rarebit—whatever that is. You?"

"Macaroni Surprise—whatever that is."

"What is a 'rarebit,' anyway? Some kind of rabbit?"

"Beats me."

Ronde smelled his food and made a face. "Man. We should've asked Mom to make us sandwiches."

"Yeah. She makes the best ones."

They picked slowly at their food, making faces. Tiki wished their mom hadn't made them be in different classes. He was sure that none of that bad stuff would have happened if Ronde'd been there with him.

Taking another bite of this "mystery meat," Ronde looked up and spotted Norman coming toward them.

Ronde spat the meat back out into his dish. "Oh, no," he said under his breath.

"What?" Tiki asked.

"Incoming."

"Hey, Ronde!" Norman greeted him. "Wait, hold on. Which one of you is—don't tell me. You're identical twins!"

"Bingo," said Ronde. He hated it when people did this. They weren't identical in everything after all—Tiki was more serious and Ronde liked to joke around more. And they argued about who was the better athlete.

"Wait, but which one's Ronde?"

"Me."

"I'm Tiki. Nice to meet you."

"Man, this is so *cool*," said Norman, not even seeing Tiki's outstretched hand. "Hey, do you guys ever pretend to, like, *be* each other? You know, like, take each other's tests and stuff?"

"Not really," Tiki said.

"'Cause you could cheat really easy and get away with it."

"You gonna sit down?" Ronde asked, ignoring his suggestion.

"No, thanks—I'm sitting with my friends. You know, from last year."

"Okay—check you out later, then."

"Yeah. Hey, if you're not gonna cheat, you really ought to do some serious studying, Ronde. Otherwise, we're *all* gonna be in trouble."

"I don't cheat," Ronde said.

"Me neither," said Tiki.

Norman shrugged. "Hey, it was just a suggestion. I cheat all the time, and no one ever knows. How do you think I knew the answer today?"

Ronde was stunned. "You really—?"

"Nah, I knew the answer. I was just messing with you. I mean, square roots? Honestly, that is so sixth grade. You embarrassed yourself today. No, wait, let me correct that—you embarrassed *all* of us. Hit the books, will ya?"

"Yeah, I'll . . . I'll do that," Ronde said, wishing he could punch Norman right in his big, loud mouth.

"Hey, man—don't talk to my brother like that!" Tiki said. "Ronde, what's he talking about?"

"Nothing," Ronde said. "Don't listen to—"

But he was too late. Norman was already telling Tiki the whole story of Ronde's terrible moment.

Tiki nodded, his face serious. "Wow," he said. "Mmm, that's rough."

After Norman had gone, Tiki looked at Ronde and said, "Hey, man, things were tough for me, too."

"They were?" Ronde felt badly for Tiki, but he was also relieved in a way. It was good to know he wasn't the only one who was having a hard time.

"Yeah, man," Tiki said. "I got hit in the head by a ball of crumpled-up paper."

"No lie?"

"I totally did. Even worse, my teacher was the one who threw it!"

"Come on."

"No lie."

"No way."

"I'm telling you! He's got a good arm, too. It came fast!" He rubbed the top of his head, frowning.

"That's pretty bad," Ronde said. "But it's not as bad as the whole class laughing at you."

"You think they didn't laugh at me?"

Ronde sighed. "Man, I'll tell you—junior high is hard."

"*Mad* hard."

"Any time you raise your hand, you can get in big trouble."

"I didn't even raise mine, and I still got creamed!" said Tiki.

"I'm *never* gonna raise *my* hand," said Ronde.

"Me neither. Man, I sure hope it gets better from here on out."

"I hear that."

Tiki touched fists with him. "I can't wait for football tryouts."

Ronde nodded, smiling for the first time in hours. "Me neither—it's gonna rock, baby!"

CHAPTER THREE

TAKE THE FIELD

RONDE GOT THROUGH HIS AFTERNOON CLASSES OKAY.
In music, everyone was busy learning a really corny song called "It's a Small, Small World," which kept repeating the same words over and over.

And in Spanish, everyone was a beginner like him. He learned how to say *"yo no sé"*—"I don't know"—something he figured would come in handy if the Spanish teacher ever called on him to answer a question.

Still, he was determined never to raise his hand again in *any* class, unless he was absolutely, positively sure he knew the answer. Being wrong was way too painful—it made you look stupid in front of everybody, and it just made it harder to raise your hand next time.

Ronde made his way to the locker room, weaving through the crowd of kids heading for the exits. *Football, at last,* he thought. *Finally!* Tiki would be there, and so would all his friends from Mews Hill—Chris, Jason, Adam, Paco . . .

Ronde was sure he and Tiki would impress the coaches. They were both natural athletes, and football was their best sport by far. They'd been standouts in Peewee League, and they would be standouts here, too.

At least, that's what Ronde thought—until he stepped into the locker room and got his first close-up look at the kids who were *already* on the team. As they changed into their well-worn Hidden Valley Eagles practice jerseys, these eighth and ninth graders looked gigantic—they had to be twice Ronde's size!

He looked around for Tiki, or anyone else he knew. Where were they all, anyway? What was keeping them?

"Hey, shrimp!" one of the big kids called out.

Ronde pretended not to hear. He put his book bag down and opened a locker to see if it was empty.

"Hey! Tiny! You hear me calling you? Turn around, baby face!"

Ronde turned around as he was ordered, and pointed to his own chest. *"Me?"*

"Yeah, you," said the enormous boy wearing the number fifty-two. He had a face pocked with pimples, and a mean look in his beady little eyes. "You see any other shrimps around here?"

"This kid giving you trouble, Bryce?" asked another humongous boy, this one wearing the number fifty-three.

"Yeah, Boomer. He's disrespecting me."

"Want me to teach him a lesson for you?"

"Nah, that's okay. I'll teach him myself—out on the practice field. What's your name, shrimp? Is it Wimpy?"

"No, it's Ronde."

"Ron-day?" Bryce said, snorting. "What kind of a name is that?"

"A weird one," said Boomer.

Bryce snorted again. "Too weird for me. I'm gonna call you Wimpy instead."

Ronde had taken about enough of this. "It's not a weird name," he insisted. "No weirder than yours."

Bryce seemed stunned for a minute. Then his face grew red with anger, and he started toward Ronde. "Okay, that's it! I don't take any noise from seventh graders."

Boomer held his friend back. "Easy, Bryce. Take it outside, like you said. Settle it on the field."

"Right," said Bryce, backing down slowly. "That's right." To Ronde, he added, "You're dead meat, Wimpy."

Just at that moment, Tiki walked into the locker room.

"Whoa!" said Boomer. "Lookie, lookie, there's two of 'em!"

"Yeah," said Bryce, flashing an evil grin. "One for me, and one for you."

Tiki looked at them, then at Ronde. "What's up?" he asked.

"We eat seventh graders for lunch," said Bryce.

Ronde's heart was pounding in his chest and echoing in his ears. Visions of Beat the Seventh Graders Day floated back into his head. Wasn't that supposed to be tomorrow, not today?

"Okay, Shrimpy and Wimpy. Get ready to get knocked flat on your behinds," said Bryce.

"Hey!" came a loud voice from behind Tiki and Ronde. "Cut it out, you turkeys. These guys might wind up being your teammates."

Ronde turned around. A tall, dark-haired boy on crutches, with a cast on his left leg, stood in the doorway.

"Yeah, right," said Boomer. "Like these two flyweights would ever make the team."

"Leave them alone," said the boy on crutches. "They've got enough on their minds today."

Tiki and Ronde looked at one another, but neither one had the nerve to say anything—not even "thanks." Instead, they got into the only practice uniforms they had—their purple Vikings jerseys from Peewee League.

"Whoa, check this out!" Bryce said, pointing and laughing. "We've got a couple of peewees here!"

"More like a couple of grapes," Boomer said.

"Yeah. How 'bout we squish 'em?" Bryce suggested.

"I said *can* it!" the boy on crutches said, glaring at Tiki and Ronde's tormentors.

There was deep silence in the locker room, with at least a dozen boys staring at them, all of them wondering what was going to happen next.

Finally, the tension broke. "Aw, we were just goofing around with 'em," said Bryce, attempting a laugh. "Don't get mad, Matt."

"Yeah, we didn't mean nothin' by it," added Boomer, as both of them backed away from the Barbers.

"Better hope not," said Matt.

Bryce and Boomer grabbed their helmets, then trotted out of the locker room and onto the practice field.

Matt limped over to the bench by Tiki and Ronde and sat down. "Hey, you guys," he said, shaking hands. "I'm Matt Clayton."

"Matt Clayton?"

Ronde knew that name—Matt Clayton was the all-conference quarterback who'd led the Eagles to a 10–2 season and the conference championship last year!

"Ronde Barber," he introduced himself. "And this is my brother, Tiki."

"Good to meet you both. And pay no attention to those two jerks. They do that to all the new kids."

Matt's comment made Ronde think again of Paco's brother, James. "Matt, could I ask you a question?" he said.

"Sure."

"Um, we heard something about this thing . . . it's called Beat the Seventh Graders Day?"

Matt laughed out loud. "Yeah, that's classic!"

"You mean . . . ?"

"It doesn't exist," Matt explained. "People just talk about it to goof on the seventh graders. It always gets the new kids so scared they start freaking out—but there's nothing to it, really."

"But our friend's brother said—"

"Aw, he was just messing with you," Matt said. "Believe me, there's nothing to it. I should know—I'm in ninth grade."

"You sure?"

"Totally. It's stupid, but don't let it get to you. Just concentrate on making the team, and don't worry about anything else. Once you've got that Eagles jersey on, you're golden around this place. Trust me."

Ronde felt a huge weight lift from his shoulders. He could tell from his brother's face that Tiki felt the same way. "Thanks, man—that's really good to know."

Matt laughed again. "And just ignore those two rock-heads. If you make the team, they'll be your best friends. I should know—I rely on them for protection when the blitz is coming."

"Is that how your leg got broken?" Tiki asked.

Matt's smile faded, and he suddenly looked sad. "Nah, I did this at camp over the summer, mountain biking. Just stupid—I shouldn't have been taking chances." He shook his head. "I'm lucky it wasn't worse. I'll be out for the first couple of games, but that's all. If you're trying out for quarterback, don't get your hopes up."

"Wait—we have to try out for just *one position*?" Ronde asked, suddenly panicking.

"Well, not really. You can try out for as many positions as you want—but they're only going to give you one, and you can't really do your best when you're trying out for a million positions."

In Peewee League, Ronde had been kick returner, wide receiver, linebacker, and defensive back. Tiki had been a running back, wide receiver, safety, and special teams player. Neither of them had ever really had a favorite position—and now they were going to have to choose just one to try out for right away!

What if they picked the wrong one?

A whistle sounded outside, and all the kids who were still changing hurried to finish dressing and get on the field.

"Well, good luck," Matt told them. "Don't try to impress anybody. Just do your best. I'll be pulling for you."

"Thanks, man," Ronde said, high-fiving him. Tiki did likewise, and the two brothers, dressed in their purple Vikings jerseys, jogged out onto the field.

"Hey, bro—that was Matt Clayton!" Tiki said as they went, giving Ronde a little shove on the shoulder. "*The* Matt Clayton!"

"I know, man—quit shoving me," Ronde said, shoving back. Laughing, the two boys headed over to the bleachers, where a crowd of players was grouped around an older man wearing a baseball cap and a green-and-gold Eagles T-shirt.

"Welcome, everybody," he said, in a loud, gravelly, penetrating voice. "I'm Coach Steve Spangler. People like to call me 'Spanky,' but don't you be doing it. To you, I'm just 'Coach.' Always 'Coach' and nothing else. Got it?"

There were a few uh-huhs, and some yesses.

"I can't *hear* you!" he shouted.

"Yes, Coach!" the boys all yelled.

"That's better. I expect you to be alert, enthusiastic, and ready for action at all times. I'm not going to say anything twice, so make sure you're 'heads-up' the first time. Got it?"

"Yes, Coach!"

"Good. Now, let's get down to business. First of all, I want to welcome back everyone who was on the team last year."

A huge cheer went up from the older boys, all of whom were wearing their Eagles practice jerseys.

"We had a great season—ten and two—and this season, we're aiming even higher. Now, do I think we can go undefeated?"

"Yeah!" shouted several of the boys.

"You bet I do!" the coach yelled, pointing back at them. "Mind you, it's never been done around here. But if we play one game at a time, and if we play each game to win, we have a definite chance to make conference history! Do I *expect* that? No—all I *expect* is that you give me 110 percent of your effort, all the time! Got it?"

"YES, COACH!!"

"All right! Now, I want to welcome all you newbies.

I know you've probably got your hands full, what with getting used to a new school and all. But football season waits for no man. We've got a game in less than two weeks, and a game every week after that for the next eleven, except for Thanksgiving weekend. So buckle up your chin straps, boys. We're gonna spend this afternoon finding out what you've got, and which of you has got what it takes to be Eagles!"

Another huge cheer rose from the crowd, with the older boys chest bumping and high-fiving all over the place.

"We've got a bunch of drill stations laid out, as you can see," said Coach Spangler. "Returning players and those trying out will work together on these drills. I'll call out your names and give you a station number to start at. You'll go through the full circuit, one drill at a time. As you'll see, we've got an assistant coach at each station to put you through your paces and give you a rating."

He began reading names off a chart. Tiki and Ronde were to start at station 3.

"Okay," said Coach Spangler as he finished. "After practice we coaches will huddle up and decide who makes the team, and at what position. The final team roster will be posted in the hallway outside the main office, first thing tomorrow morning—so don't ask us *today* if you made the team or not."

He tucked his clipboard under his arm. "But I'll tell you this: we've got fifty kids trying out. And with the rest of the team returning, we've only twenty open slots to fill. So as you can see, more than half you new kids are going to be disappointed. But try not to get too down—there are always the intramural teams.

"Even those of you who make the squad probably won't be starting, so don't get your hopes up too high. Just do your best, and let us coaches make the decisions. Okay, here we go!"

He blew his whistle three times. The crowd of boys scattered. As Ronde and Tiki made their way to station 3, Ronde waved to Matt Clayton, sitting in the bleachers. Matt waved back—but he didn't smile.

Ronde thought he knew why. It had to be tough sitting on the bench after having been a star last year. He felt sorry for Matt—but right now Ronde had a job to do—he had to make the team!

At station 3, blocking dummies were set up in a row. One by one, the boys had to get into set position, rush the dummies, and hit them. On Ronde's first turn, he hit the dummy going full speed. It bent back a little, but it was so hard to move that it wound up throwing Ronde backward! He landed on his rear end, and had to dust himself off as the other boys laughed.

Pretty much the same thing happened to Tiki—the Barber boys were among the shortest, skinniest kids trying out for the team. Ronde couldn't help thinking they weren't cut out to be linemen. Their blocking technique was good, but they weren't as big and strong as the other boys.

Next, the boys lined up in rows opposite each other. "Okay, boys," said the coach who was manning the station, "we're going to take turns being defensive and offensive linemen. This row will start on defense. Your job is to get around the offense. Offense, try to block them."

Ronde looked up to see Boomer staring at him, grinning. "Get ready, little guy," he told Ronde. "Here I come."

Twice in a row, Boomer flattened Ronde as he plowed right through him. Then Ronde had an idea. On the third rush, when Boomer came at him, Ronde used Boomer's own momentum against him, throwing him forward instead of trying to stop him. This time, it was Boomer who landed flat on the ground!

Boomer got up slowly, looking angrily at Ronde. "Think you're pretty smart, huh?" he said. "Try that again, and see what happens."

Luckily, the coach had them switch sides then. On offense, Ronde was fast and tricky enough to get around Boomer.

"Not bad, kid," Boomer nodded when they were done. "You've got pretty good moves there. Maybe you ought to be running back punts and kickoffs instead."

The next station was for agility drills. There were rope squares laid out in a grid, and you had to use fancy footwork to get through the grid fast, without hitting the ropes or missing a box.

Ronde had done this drill before, and he loved it. He got through the squares in the blink of an eye, and he could tell he had made a good impression on the coach who was timing them.

Then Tiki did the drill even faster! "Hey, we've got a pair of studs here!" the coach said, staring at his stopwatch. Tiki and Ronde exchanged a thumbs-up. Things were starting to look better.

They threw passes, ran routes, took handoffs, punted, and performed on special teams. They were timed on sprints, and had their weight and height measured.

"Can you *believe* all this?" Tiki whispered while they waited their turn for the forty-yard dash.

"I know," said Ronde. "It's awesome!"

While waiting, Ronde had been taking a good look around the field, to see what some of the other kids were doing. He watched excitedly as Paco put a ninth-grade defender on his rear end with a ferocious headfirst tackle, then rushed the quarterback and touched him for a sack.

Go, Paco! Ronde said to himself. *Show 'em who's boss!*

Looking over to station 1, he winced as Jason overthrew two straight passes. *What is the matter with him?* Ronde wondered. *Why can't he hit the mark like he has in Peewee League, or even on Mews Hill Drive?*

Jason looked like he'd been punched in the gut. His shoulders slumped as he trudged over to his next station.

Ronde felt awful for him. Quarterback was Jason's only position! If he didn't make it there, would he even make the team at all?

At station 4, Adam was hopeless, getting yelled at every time he tripped on the rope squares. And there was Chris, back at station 1, dropping every pass thrown to him, as if his hands had been smeared with butter.

"Man," Ronde said quietly to Tiki, "it sure looks like a lot of our friends are choking in the clutch. What's up with that?"

"Yeah, that's messed up," Tiki agreed.

"Paco looks good, though."

"That's good, but never mind them. How do you think *we're* doing?"

"Hey, you two! Quiet over there!"

Rats! Now one of the coaches was ticked at both of them! Ronde wondered if that would hurt their chances.

Tiki was still staring at him, waiting for an answer to his question. *How do you think we're doing?*

Ronde didn't speak. He just bit his lip and shrugged, as if to say, *I don't know, man—and I'm afraid to find out.*

CHAPTER FOUR

ANTICIPATION

TRYOUTS WERE LONG OVER, AND THEY WERE ON THE late bus home. "You never answered my question," Tiki said.

"What question?"

"How do you think we did? You think we made it?"

"Of course we made it!" Ronde said. "Are you kidding me? We were the best new guys there!"

"You sure?"

"Sure I'm sure!"

But Ronde didn't look sure at all. "Aren't *you* sure?" he asked.

"Sure . . . I guess." Truth was, Tiki wasn't the least bit sure.

Yes, they were fast, and athletic, and talented. But so were a lot of the other kids trying out. Tiki remembered some of them from Peewee League. But others were new to him. They'd come to Hidden Valley from schools in other neighborhoods—and a lot of them were *good*.

Back home, their mom was waiting for them at the front door with a hopeful smile on her face. "How did the first day of school go, you two?"

Tiki and Ronde looked at each other, to see who was going to answer first. Neither one wanted to. "It went okay, I guess," Ronde said.

"Not too bad," Tiki agreed.

Mrs. Barber frowned. "Well, that's not exactly a ringing thumbs-up," she said. "Come on inside and have dinner, and you can tell me all about it."

She had their dinner waiting for them. While they ate, they told her all about their different classes—leaving out the most embarrassing parts, of course.

"And how were tryouts for the team?" she asked.

"Oh—they went good," Tiki said.

"They went *well*," Mrs. Barber corrected him.

"Yes, ma'am."

"I'm glad to hear that."

"Ma," Ronde said, "after we eat, can we go out and play football with the guys?"

"After you eat *and* do your *homework*," said their mom. "You do have homework, don't you?"

Tiki wished he could have said he didn't, but that would have been a lie. Holding back the truth from his mom was bad enough—but lying to her face would have been much worse.

• • •

By the time their homework was done, it was almost seven o'clock. Still, it was only early September, and the sun hadn't set yet. So, the boys grabbed their football and headed outside. Adam, Chris, and Jason were already there, sitting on the curb. "Where've you guys been?" Jason asked. "It's gonna be dark pretty soon."

"We had to do our homework first," Ronde explained.

"Why couldn't you just do it later?" Jason asked.

"You know Mom won't let us," Tiki said.

"Man," Jason said. "That's harsh."

"We know there's no use in trying to get around it," Tiki said. "And anyway, maybe there's something to it— we get As and Bs, and you get Cs."

"Shut up," Jason said, frowning.

Tiki blinked in surprise. He'd only been joking about the Cs, but Jason had taken him seriously. Tiki could see his friend was in a seriously bad mood.

"I stunk it up today," Jason said. "I'm not gonna make the team."

"Sure you are!" Tiki said. "We *all* are!"

"I don't know," Chris said. "I kind of stunk too."

"Hey, everybody made mistakes today," Ronde said. "We were all nervous. I was—and so was Tiki."

"Speak for yourself, yo," Tiki said, grinning and poking Ronde in the arm.

"Come on, you know you were shaking in your shoes," Ronde shot back.

Suddenly, all of them stopped talking at once. Mrs. Pendergast was coming down the street toward them.

Mrs. Pendergast was a lady who dressed in clothes from the distant past. At least, they looked that way. Her wild gray hair was piled up on top of her head, and some of it kept trying to escape in all directions.

Mrs. Pendergast talked to herself a lot. All the kids on the block were scared of her, even though she was nice to them, always giving them a smile and a big "Hello!"

Tiki and Ronde both thought she was one of the weirdest people they'd ever met. But their mother always said, "She's a little different from most people, but she has a heart of gold."

"Hello, boys!" Mrs. Pendergast said as she passed by.

"Hi, Mrs. Pendergast," Tiki and Ronde said.

Their friends said nothing—they just watched as Mrs. Pendergast continued down the street, mumbling to herself. Then she made a sharp left turn—and headed straight for the Barbers' front door!

Tiki and Ronde looked at each other, wide-eyed. Mrs. Pendergast was ringing their doorbell—*and their mom was letting her in*!

Mrs. Pendergast loved to talk. Whenever they met her on the street, Tiki and Ronde had to wait forever while she talked to their mom about this and that.

Still, she had never been *inside their house* before. Tiki

wondered what she wanted, and why it was so important that she had to come over to talk about it.

Paco showed up, having finished his homework too. The boys played some more football, and spent some time going back over what they'd done well or poorly at tryouts. More than anything, they wanted to get it right.

After about half an hour Mrs. Pendergast came out of the Barber house and headed home, just down the block.

"Hello again!" she chirped as she passed the boys.

"Hi," Tiki and Ronde said, while their friends just stared.

They played ball for another few minutes. It was still light out, but now the other boys had to go home and get their homework done. "If you would have done it first, like Paco and us, we could still be playing!" Tiki pointed out to them—but none of them wanted to hear it.

"Save it, Tiki," Jason said. "You sound just like a grown-up."

Later Tiki noticed that his mom seemed distracted, staring into space a lot. "What did Mrs. Pendergast want, Ma?" he asked her.

"I'm glad you asked, Tiki," she said. "It's so disturbing, I can't stop thinking about it."

"What is it?" Tiki asked.

"Mrs. Pendergast is weird," Ronde said.

"Well, thank goodness for people like her, is all I can say," their mom said. "And you two should be grateful she lives around here. Do you know what she told me today? There's a big corporation that wants to build a factory right at the end of Mews Hill Drive—that's only six blocks from here!"

"So?" Ronde said. "What's wrong with that? Won't it give people jobs?"

"Well, yes," their mom said. "But this factory will also pollute the air and water in our neighborhood. The corporation says it'll be within safe levels, but Mrs. Pendergast showed me articles that say it isn't going to be safe at all!"

"Ma," said Tiki, "they wouldn't let them *build* a factory around here if it was going to hurt people."

"Tiki," she said, "I wish that were always true. Sometimes, money becomes more important than people. But people don't have to let things happen to them—it's a free country, and we can always speak our minds."

"What are you going to do, Ma?" Ronde asked.

"Mrs. Pendergast told me that the district council has to approve the factory. She's going to go to the open council meeting and complain. And I'm going with her!"

"Ma, don't!" Tiki said. "People will think you're weird."

"Why? Because I'm with Mrs. Pendergast?"

"Yes!" Ronde said. "And because . . . because . . ."

"Because why, Ronde?"

"Because if you stand up and say stuff in front of all those people, they'll all know what you *think*."

"Yeah," Tiki agreed. "Let Mrs. Pendergast do it. Everybody already thinks *she's* weird."

"Boys," said their mom, "sometimes we all have to stand up and be counted, even speak our minds. I hope that when you're older, you'll do the same. I'm going to stand up and speak my mind. And you're both coming with me."

"*What?*" the boys both jumped up from the table at the same instant.

"Bring your homework along in case it goes long," she added, smiling slyly.

"Aw, Ma!"

The last thing Tiki wanted was to be shown off with his twin to a room full of grown-ups. He and Ronde were way too old for that—they were in junior high school now!

But he also knew that when his mom made up her mind about something, nothing could change it. If she wanted them to attend some boring council meeting, the boys would just have to grit their teeth and go.

Tiki barely slept, but when the alarm went off, he was out of bed and into his clothes and shoes in less than thirty seconds.

He couldn't wait to see whether he'd made the team!

He didn't even want to think about not being on that list—it would be a total disaster! And though he thought he'd done okay at tryouts, he certainly hadn't shown them his best.

The list had been haunting his dreams all night. Three times, he'd woken up in a sweat when his name or Ronde's wasn't on it. He had looked over to see his brother tossing and turning too.

And now it was morning and they were on their way to school to read the list *for real.*

Neither Tiki nor Ronde said much as they walked slowly up the steps to the main entrance. They might as well have been walking to final exams.

Tiki was practically shaking with fear. He knew Ronde was going through the same thing. That should have made things easier, but instead it made it twice as hard.

There it was! Tiki saw the list posted on the wall in front of the main office, just as Coach Spangler had promised. A crowd of boys was already stationed in front of it, each one looking frantically for his own name. Some yelled "Yes!" and jumped in the air when they found they were on the list. Others muttered angrily, or just looked down at the floor and walked away, their hearts broken.

Tiki and Ronde bulled their way to the front, using what felt like every ounce of their strength to break through the crowd. Tiki could see Jason, Adam, Paco, and Chris, all grouped in the front row, staring upward.

"Hey, Jason, there you are!" Paco shouted, pointing.

"Yeah, baby!" Jason said, pumping his fist and high-fiving Paco. "You and me, dude! I knew we'd make it!"

Tiki panicked for a second. Why hadn't they mentioned him or Ronde?

At that moment, Paco saw them. "Yo, dudes, we're in!" he said, his hands raised for high-fiving.

Tiki felt a huge weight fall from his shoulders. He could breathe again! Still, he looked up and down the list, just to make sure Paco was right.

Yes, there he and Ronde were—*whew!*

"I made it too, and so did Jason!" Paco said, throwing his arms around the Barbers. "Man, we are gonna rock this conference!"

"Did you guys make it?" Tiki asked Adam and Chris.

Jason replied for them. "Adam's in—check this out!" He pointed to the bottom right corner of the list, where Adam was listed under "kicker."

"Incredible, man!" Tiki said, giving Adam the Mews Hill handshake. "I saw you out there, kicking the hide off that ball. That's awesome!"

"Yeah," Adam said with a shy grin. "Coach told me to concentrate on special teams. He said I had a golden leg." He laughed softly. "He even asked me if it was bionic!"

"And what about you?" Ronde asked Chris.

Chris shook his head. "Nah."

"Aw, man, that really *hurts*," Paco said. "I mean, all of us makin' it, but not you? Sorry, man."

"It's okay," Chris said, shrugging. "I really don't care about it that much."

"Yeah, right," Jason said. "It's okay to feel bad, dude. Sometimes things just don't go the right way."

"No, I'm serious," said Chris. He pulled a bunch of flyers out of his book bag. "I'm already joining the debating team, and Model U.N., and I'm in Scouts, too. Tell you the truth, I wasn't sure I was going to have time for this anyway."

Tiki felt better knowing Chris wasn't too down about not making the team. All the rest of that day, he was floating on a cloud, and he knew the others must be feeling the same way. He couldn't wait for practice that afternoon!

A couple of times Mr. Wheeler called on him when he wasn't paying attention, and the whole class laughed when he got drilled with the crumpled paper ball again. Tiki winced, knowing he was probably getting a reputation as a space cadet.

Still, the thought of football practice kept him happy and excited. When the final bell rang, he raced for the locker room, dodging kids in the hallway left and right.

It was only when he sat down in front of his locker that he remembered—today was supposed to have been Beat the Seventh Graders Day! The whole day had gone by, and Tiki hadn't even realized it! He couldn't help laughing, to think how scared he'd been.

Ronde showed up just then, and said, "What's so funny?"

Tiki told him, and both boys laughed together. When Paco arrived, they gave him a hard time about it, too. "Yo, man, what happened to the big, bad ninth graders?" Ronde asked him.

Paco was steaming. "Man, I'm gonna beat James up so bad," he said, his hands balling into fists.

"Yeah, right," Ronde said. "Like that'll ever happen."

"What, you think I couldn't take him?" Paco challenged.

"Paco," said Tiki, "James is like fifty pounds heavier than you, and it's all muscle. If I were you, I'd let it go."

Paco pounded his locker with his fist, but Tiki knew he'd never pick a fight with James. Paco wasn't the brightest kid in the world, but he wasn't *that* stupid.

Matt Clayton limped into the locker room on his crutches. He was wearing his number twenty-one Eagles jersey, but without any padding. "Yo, wuzzup?" he called out. Everyone let out a whoop, welcoming last year's hero back to the team.

Bryce and Boomer walked in together. "Yo, rookies!" they called out, coming over to Tiki, Ronde, and the other seventh graders. "Give it up!" They high-fived and chest bumped everyone, making funny comments as they went.

"Don't worry, Shrimpy and Wimpy—we've got your backs."

"Yo, you looked good on that long bomb yesterday, Ronde. You a wide receiver?" Boomer asked.

"I don't know," Ronde answered. "Maybe."

"You're James's brother, right?" Bryce asked Paco. "What's your name again?"

"Paco."

"Paco? You're some sack of cement, dude. Welcome to the offensive line."

"Welcome to the once and future champions!" Boomer boomed, true to his name.

Tiki tried to chest bump Bryce, but he had to jump pretty high, because Bryce was six inches taller.

"Don't worry, little dude," Bryce told him. "You probably haven't hit your growth spurt yet."

It was the same kind of comment he'd made yesterday—but today, it sounded totally different. They were *teammates* now. Tiki felt a warm glow all over just thinking about it. They were *all* teammates!

Assistant coaches came around, giving out uniforms and helmets. Tiki was handed jersey number one. Ronde got number five.

When he was all dressed, Tiki trotted outside. Most of the others were already there, surrounding Head Coach Spangler.

"All right, welcome to the Eagles, all you new guys," he said. "And welcome back, you upperclassmen. As most of you know, this is a team with a long and glorious history—including two championships in the past ten years. And I'm confident that this will be the year we make new history, and repeat as conference champs!"

A huge cheer went up from all the Eagles. When it died down, Coach Spangler continued.

"Now, the next two practices, today's and tomorrow's, are designed to help me and the other coaches figure out who plays where, and to firm up the starting lineups. So you new kids, this is your chance to show us everything you've got. On Monday, we'll post the list of who's starting, who's second-string and third-string. Our season opener's next week, so let's not waste any more time, shall we?"

Once practice got started, Tiki found himself feeling tense. Normally, he was free and easy on the football field, sure of his talent and having fun playing the game. But today, he could feel his heart pounding, and hear it pounding in his ears.

He dropped easy passes he normally caught. He tried to make cuts that were too tight, and wound up slipping and falling on his face. On defense, he let a touchdown be completed right over his outstretched fingertips.

When practice was over, he found Ronde. "How'd you do?" he asked his twin.

"Not too good. You?"

"About the same."

"I don't know what happened to me," Ronde said. "I stunk."

"Me too. You think Coach might change his mind and kick us off the team?"

"No way!" Ronde said quickly. "I mean . . . I don't think so. Do you?"

"Nah," said Tiki. But he had to wonder.

As the two boys passed the sidelines, Matt Clayton called them over.

"Hey, you two," he said. "Don't get down. There's still tomorrow."

"But we skunked it up," Ronde said.

"We stunk," Tiki agreed.

"Listen," Matt said, "quit trying so hard to impress the coaches. Just do your thing, and trust them to notice. You guys are talented enough, okay? Don't get down—just learn from your mistakes."

"I don't know," Ronde said, shaking his head.

Matt gave them both a pat on the shoulder. "Just remember, you guys—it's all about the *team*. Success starts with the right attitude."

"What do you mean?" Tiki asked.

"Quit trying to be solo superstars, okay? Think about the team, and it will happen."

The words stung, but deep down, Tiki knew Matt was right. The thing was, could he and Ronde go out on the field tomorrow and really *do* it?

CHAPTER FIVE

MOM RULES

"YES, YOU DO HAVE TO COME!" MRS. BARBER SAID. She stood in the open doorway, one hand on the door-knob, the other holding her purse—the fancy one she took with her when it was a special occasion.

"Aw, Ma!" Ronde stomped the carpet with his foot, but it didn't impress her. Tantrums never did.

Ronde pulled at the starched collar that was itching his neck. It was hot to be wearing long-sleeved white shirts and ties, but their mom had insisted. They were coming with her to this stupid district council meeting whether they liked it or not, because she said it was important.

"If you don't understand why," she told them, "you will afterward." That was all she would say about it.

Mrs. Pendergast was waiting for them, outside, in her rusty, crusty old car. "Hi!" she greeted them. "Hop in!'

Mrs. Pendergast sure seemed cheerful. *Sure*, thought Ronde. *Why shouldn't she be happy? She's got my mom on her side.*

Ronde and Tiki were not cheerful—not at all. Paco and Jason were sitting on the curb and saw them go. It was embarrassing to be seen by all the guys going out all dressed up with your mom and Mrs. Pendergast—the weirdest lady in town! Why couldn't Mom have driven?

They pulled into the parking lot at the local library and went inside. Tiki and Ronde tried to stay a few feet in back of their mother and Mrs. Pendergast.

There were nine people sitting behind a big long desk. They had microphones and their names on plaques in front of them. Ronde knew that these were the men and women of the council—the ones his mom wanted to talk to.

There weren't very many other people in the room when a man their mom said was the clerk banged his gavel down and started the meeting. A few more came in while the council dealt with other things. Then it was time to discuss the planned new factory.

"We will now have our public comment period. Would anyone like to speak?"

Mrs. Pendergast went first. Ronde didn't listen too closely to what she said, but he could see she was very angry about the factory. She was almost yelling at the council, and Ronde could tell they didn't like that. They were all frowning at her.

Two other people also spoke—more softly, thank goodness. Then Mrs. Barber stood up, and went to the public microphone in the center of the room.

"My name is Geraldine Barber," she said. "I live on Mews Hill Drive, only six blocks away from the site. And

I think it is a shame that there aren't more people here—
more people who are worried about this factory, and afraid
of what will happen if it's built. I have two boys myself,"
she said, and put her hand out toward Tiki and Ronde.

Everyone in the room looked at them. A few people in
the audience even applauded. Ronde looked down at the
floor, and out of the corner of his eye, he could see Tiki
doing the same thing.

"I want to hear more about this factory before you go
and let them build it," she said. "I think it's a shame more
people didn't know about this meeting—but you didn't
let them know ahead of time!"

All at once, everyone in the audience got up and
applauded. Ronde couldn't believe it! The clerk banged
his gavel, but nobody stopped clapping.

The clerk finally hammered the room into silence.
Then the council president spoke. "Very well," she said.
"I move that we allow another public comment session
before deciding on the application to build the factory.
All in favor, say 'aye.'"

Five council members said 'aye.' Four said 'nay.'
The people in the audience stood up and cheered again,
applauding Mrs. Barber.

On the way out, Tiki and Ronde each held one of her
hands. Everyone congratulated them—the boys, too, as if
they'd done something. But Ronde was so proud of his
mother right then, he could have burst.

"You boys understand now?" she asked them.

"Uh-huh," they both said.

She wasn't smiling, though, and Ronde thought she looked worried. "What's wrong, Ma?" he asked. "Didn't everything go good?"

"Go *well*," she corrected him. "No, it didn't go well, Ronde."

"But—"

"They gave us one more chance, is all—one chance to show them that people are against this factory being built. And it's up to us to show them."

"Us?"

"Me and Mrs. Pendergast, and the other people who showed up tonight. Believe me, the council isn't going to put up billboards advertising the next meeting. It's going to be up to us."

"What are you going to do, Ma?" Tiki asked.

"I may not be a big muckety-muck," she said, "but I've got friends—lots of friends, people I know—and they all know people too. I'm going to see to it that we have a hundred folks at that next meeting, and a thousand more names on a petition to stop that factory!"

Now Ronde wasn't so happy. Sure, he was proud of his mom, but he was also worried. Mrs. Pendergast would be coming over to their house all the time now—and all the kids would know it.

• • •

As he suited up for practice the next afternoon, Ronde remembered what Matt Clayton had said to him and Tiki. "It's all about the *team* . . ."

Today, he would try to follow that advice. He'd gotten nowhere the day before, trying to impress the coaches with great plays. He'd fumbled trying to gain an extra yard, and he'd blown coverages twice on defense when he'd tried for spectacular interceptions.

"You thinking what I'm thinking?" Tiki asked him.

"Uh-huh," said Ronde. "It's all about the team."

"That's right. Okay, let's go get 'em!"

They ran out onto the field together, and lined up for drills. Ronde somehow felt more focused than the day before. Was it because of what Matt had said? Or was it the way his mom had stood tall the night before?

Whatever it was, today Ronde kept things simple. He didn't make any mistakes, and he took advantage of every chance he got to make a play.

In that day's scrimmage, he and Tiki were on the same side, with Tiki running the ball on offense, and Ronde playing linebacker on defense. Tiki scored a sixty-yard touchdown, breaking three tackles on the way to the end zone. And Ronde had a sack, a forced fumble, and an interception.

"Man, that was like our dream game!" Tiki said as they trotted off the field at the end of practice. "You know, like the ones we play on the street, except we didn't have Chris to do the sportscast!"

"Yeah," Ronde said with a nervous laugh. "Too bad it wasn't a real game."

Still, he felt good about their chances. If those coaches had been watching, and he was sure they had, he and Tiki were definitely going to be starters.

Unless, of course, Coach Spangler had meant what he said the other day—that most of the new kids would be second- and third-stringers this season.

"You guys rocked!" Jason said, clapping them both on the back in the locker room.

"You too, man," Tiki told him.

It was true, Ronde thought as he high-fived his friend. Jason had quarterbacked their scrimmage team, throwing two awesome bombs and scrambling for a big first down.

On the way home, when their teammates were out of earshot, Jason said, "I figure you guys'll be at least second-string. But I'll bet I get to start at quarterback, at least until Matt Clayton's leg heals up."

"What? You don't think *we'll* get to start?" Tiki asked.

"I don't think so," Jason said. "Coach Spangler said—"

"I know what he said," Tiki said, "but did you *see* us today?"

"Sure I did. You guys were awesome."

"Yeah," said Tiki, still annoyed. "You got that right."

"Well, never mind," said Ronde. "Monday morning, we'll all know for sure."

When Ronde and Tiki got home, no one was there. Mrs. Barber had left them a note on the kitchen table: *Mrs. P. and I are out knocking on doors. Dinner is in the fridge. Love, Mom.*

The boys ate their dinner—warmed-over chicken with rice and beans—and did their homework. Ronde and Tiki closed their last book at exactly the same time.

"What time is it?" Ronde asked.

"Eight thirty."

"Is that all? Hey, Tiki, what do you say we go visit our fort?"

"You serious?" Tiki said. "We haven't been there since we were little kids."

"You mean like last year?"

"What are you talking about, man? It was at least two years ago."

"So all I'm saying is, how about we go there right now?"

"Aw, man, it's dark out. How are we even going to find it?"

"Ever hear of a flashlight?"

Their old fort was really just a bunch of broken brick walls from a building that had burned down a long time ago. It sat in an empty lot, where tall grass hid the fort from the street.

It was a secret place—*their* secret place. Paco had been there a few times, of course, and Adam, too, once or twice—but mostly, it was Fort Barber.

The stars were out tonight in full force. And from the fort, you could even see the big neon star on top of Mill Mountain, overlooking the whole city and shining in red, white, and blue. Crickets chirped loudly, covering the muffled sound of their voices.

"Tiki?"

"Yeah?"

"How do you think it's going?"

"What?"

"You know—everything. School, like that."

"Well, we didn't get beat up. That was good."

"True."

"On the other hand, I wish we had our classes together, like before."

"Me too," said Ronde. "I used to raise my hand more then."

"Me too."

"You think Mom was right, separating us like that?"

Tiki shrugged. "I don't know. I guess we do have to get used to it sooner or later anyway."

"It didn't have to be *now*," Ronde said. "I mean, don't you sometimes wish she didn't get all those ideas in her head?"

"What, you mean like about that factory?"

"Well, yeah. What if she gets up at the next meeting and everybody boos her?"

"Or yells at her."

"Yeah. Or even throws stuff at her!"

"If Mrs. Pendergast starts yelling again, they might!"

The boys had scared themselves into silence. Finally, Tiki broke it. "So what about you?"

"Huh?"

"You never said whether you like the school."

"I don't know. There's not a lot of kids I know, and that's hard. I mean, I used to know everybody."

"Yeah."

"You like the school?"

"I guess it depends."

"On what?"

Tiki was silent for a moment. "You think we'll get to start?" he asked.

"I wish I knew," Ronde said. "It would be great if we're starters."

"Yeah, but what if we aren't?"

Ronde knew what Tiki was trying to say—life at school would be great if they were starters on the team. But second-stringers didn't play all that much. And third-stringers barely got in the games at all. If that happened, life at school would be a nightmare!

"What's the worst that could happen?" Ronde asked.

"We could be third-stringers, and never get into the games except in garbage time."

"I can think of something even worse than that," Ronde said.

"What could be worse than that?"

"If one of us is a starter, and the other is a third-stringer."

The crickets chirped loudly in the silence between the boys.

"Well, we'll know soon," Ronde finally said.

"Yeah. Monday morning."

"Yeah."

CHAPTER SIX

ALL SHOOK UP

MONDAY MORNING DAWNED SUNNY AND BRIGHT. Tiki took that as a good sign. As he and Ronde rode the bus to school, both boys were quiet. But Tiki was confident they would both be starters—and he could tell Ronde felt the same way.

And why shouldn't they be starters? Didn't they leave it all on the field at both practices? Oh, sure, they'd made plenty of mistakes. But at the last practice, they'd both made a big impression, no question about it.

There was the usual big knot of kids standing in front of the list. Most of them looked to be seventh graders— they would look up, find their name, and for most of them, their shoulders would sink as they found out they were going to be backups.

Tiki led the way, threading through the crowd toward the front, with Ronde right behind him. "You ready?" he asked.

"Ready as I'll ever be." Ronde gulped.

Tiki looked up. There was his name, near the top and right below Ronde's. He looked at the center column: It said, "Running back."

Cool!

Then he continued across to the right-hand column:

"Third team."

Third team?

"What?" he cried. "That's no fair!"

"Man!" Ronde said, shaking his head. Next to his name, it said, "Secondary—third team."

After all they had shown the coaches, this was the reward they got? "I can't believe this!" Tiki blurted out.

"Maybe it's a mistake," Ronde said hopefully. But somehow inside he didn't think so.

"Yeah, right," Tiki said, suddenly feeling a lump rising in his throat. "It's a mistake, all right. Look at all the others—almost everybody's third-string."

Ronde looked all the way down the list. "Hey, check this out—Paco's a starter!"

"Huh?"

Tiki looked to where his twin was pointing. Sure enough, next to Paco's name, it said, "Offensive tackle—first team."

"Now you tell me, what about us?" Ronde asked. "Is that fair? Nothing against Paco, but you know we're better than he is at football. We've been playing together for years."

"I *know*," Tiki moaned.

"And look here—Adam's a starter too!"

"What!" Tiki was stunned. Adam was a great hitter

in baseball, but everyone in their group of friends knew football wasn't his game. Yet there he was, listed as first-string kicker.

"This is so wrong." Ronde said angrily. "Man, these coaches are blind!"

"You got that right," Tiki said.

"Oh, so now we're *blind*?" came a man's deep voice behind them.

Tiki spun around, and saw that Mr. Pellugi, who was his Health Ed teacher, and also one of the Eagles' defensive coaches, was standing right there.

"Uh, no! I didn't say that," Ronde stammered. "I mean, yeah, I said it, but I didn't mean it—I mean . . . I meant . . ."

"Look," said Coach Pellugi, "it wasn't easy making all these decisions. Mostly, Coach Spangler just puts all the seventh graders on the third team, unless we're thin at a particular position. You'll get your chance. Football is a game of patience."

Tiki could see where a kid might make the first team at kicker and offensive line, because not that many kids had tried out for them. Or maybe the first-teamers at those positions had all graduated, opening spots for new kids.

"Just hang in there, boys," said Coach Pellugi. "You'll get your chance to play." He walked into the office, leaving the group of disappointed boys standing there.

That was when Jason showed up. "Yo, dudes!" he said, a big smile on his face. "Did you make the starting team?"

Tiki and Ronde looked down at the floor and shook their heads.

"Aw, man . . . Well, don't take it too hard. Not everybody can be a starter right off the bat."

He looked up at the list, checking for his own name. Then he found it. *"Third team,"* he cried. "No way! No *possible* way!"

Jason's usually pale face got as red as a chili pepper. He slammed his book bag on the ground. The zipper popped open, and all his books scattered across the floor, but he didn't even bother to pick them up.

"This stinks so bad!" he said, pounding on the list with his fist. "Man, I am *not* riding the bench for the whole season, just so I can watch some other kid play quarterback just because he's an eighth grader!"

"But Jason," Tiki began, "you just said we should be patient—"

"Yeah, well, I take it all back," said Jason. "That's for *losers*. Not for me."

"Jason, what else can we do but be patient?" Ronde asked. "That's just the way it is."

"Not for *me* it isn't," said Jason. "I was the best quarterback at both practices. And don't give me that 'Matt Clayton' baloney. He is still in a cast. I should have been the starter, hands down, and you know it!"

"Hey, man, chill out," Tiki advised him. "Quit making a scene, all right?"

Teachers were popping their heads out of the office to see what all the commotion was about.

"*You* chill out," Jason said, kicking his book bag one more time before bending down to gather up his stuff. "I'm outta here."

"Huh?"

"I quit this stupid team," Jason said, stuffing his books and papers back into his bag any which way. "I'm gonna try out for some other team, where I'll actually get to play. If you two idiots want to put up with this garbage, go ahead. That's your problem."

He stormed off down the hall, just as the early bell rang, warning everyone that it was time to head to first period classes.

"Whoa," Ronde said. "I've never seen Jason so ticked off."

"No lie," Tiki agreed. "Hey, man—you think he's right?"

Ronde shook his head. "I know how he feels, though. I mean, it's embarrassing—Adam and Paco make the starting team, and we're all riding the bench?"

"I hear you." Tiki didn't know how he was ever going to face Adam and Paco. Even worse, he couldn't bear the idea of showing up for games just to sit on the bench the whole game.

Today was already the worst day of his life, Tiki thought. And it was only just beginning!

His football dreams were ruined. If he and Ronde couldn't even make *second* team, let alone first, how were they ever going to make it all the way to the NFL?

"Maybe Jason's right," Ronde said. "Maybe we should quit the team. I mean, if we tried out for soccer, or lacrosse or something, we could probably start right away."

"Soccer? Lacrosse?"

"Yeah, man, they're pretty cool—and not that many kids try out."

Tiki shook his head. "Ronde, when we sit around thinking about what we want to do when we grow up, we don't think about playing pro soccer."

Ronde sighed. "No, I guess not."

"Does pro lacrosse even exist? I don't think so."

"Doubt it."

"Maybe we should just chill out. Remember what Coach Pellugi said—and Matt Clayton, too. Let's just be patient, and hope we'll get our chance sooner or later."

Ronde shook his head. "Whatever," he said. "But it had better be sooner, not later."

The boys walked off in silence. What more was there to say?

It was another bad day at school, naturally. It had been a terrible, terrible week, and today was the worst day of all—*Friday*.

Usually, Friday was the best day of the school week, with the whole weekend to look forward to. But not this week. Tomorrow was Saturday—and the first game of the Eagles' season.

In class, concentrating was impossible. Only in Mr. Wheeler's class, where he feared being hit by flying paper balls, was Tiki able to buckle down and pay attention. And when the school day was finally over, Tiki could tell by the look on his brother's face that things hadn't gone too well for him either.

At practice Tiki and Ronde went through all their paces, but their hearts weren't in it, and their weak effort showed. The coaches were constantly urging them to do more, to try harder. But nothing seemed to help.

Once they got home, the boys were in no rush to do their homework. They didn't even *want* to go out and play, because that meant playing *football*—and even *thinking* about football was painful. It only reminded them of their failure to make the starting team!

Tiki played with his pencil and protractor. He drew doodles. Homework time seemed longer than football practice time. The doorbell rang, but neither Tiki nor Ronde cared to answer it.

Their mom did. "Paco's here to see you," she said.

"Tell him we're sick," Ronde said.

"What?"

"We don't feel good, Mom," Tiki said. It was the truth, too. He felt like absolute crud. He just didn't feel like talking about why.

"Don't feel *well*, you mean," Mrs. Barber corrected him. "Here, let me feel your foreheads."

But the boys didn't have fevers. They were sick to their stomachs, and had a bitter taste in their mouths—a taste even Mom's chicken soup couldn't cure.

"Well, I've got to go out after dinner," said Mrs. Barber.

"Where are you going, Ma?" Tiki asked. "Out with Mrs. Pendergast again?"

"Not tonight," she said. "Tonight's Back to School Night."

"Already?" Ronde gasped.

"But it's only the second week!" Tiki said in a scared voice.

"Sooner the better," Mrs. Barber said. "I'm anxious to see what Hidden Valley Junior High is all about."

What she didn't say—but both Tiki and Ronde knew—was that she also wanted to ask their teachers how the twins were doing in class.

Uh-oh . . .

It was nearly ten o'clock at night when the front door opened and closed.

"Ma?" Tiki called from the living room sofa where he and Ronde were sitting, watching the NFL report on TV.

Nobody answered.

"Ma, is that you?" Ronde called.

She appeared in the doorway, frowning. "Well!" she said, coming slowly into the room and dropping down in her favorite armchair. "Did I ever get an earful tonight!"

"What do you mean, Ma?" Ronde asked innocently. But he knew what was coming.

"I found out that most of your teachers don't even know who you are!" she said. "Apparently, you never raise your hands in class, you seem not to be paying attention, and you show no interest in learning anything. Both of you!"

"That's not true, Mom!" Tiki protested.

"We were just distracted," Ronde explained.

"Oh, really? By what?"

"By the football team," Tiki said. "But that's all over now, Ma, so you don't have to worry about it anymore."

"'All over'? What do you mean, 'all over'?"

Tiki and Ronde told their mom the awful truth: They were *losers*. Big-time losers—third-stringers, while their friends were starters! Their big dream of starring in the Super Bowl together was dead and buried. They'd never even make it to the Eagles' starting lineup, let alone the NFL!

"Now, boys," said their mother, "you need to start paying attention—in and out of class. When people tell you to wait for your chance, and to be ready when it comes, you ought to listen! When teachers share their knowledge with you, you ought to be grateful and interested. Maybe you don't think what they're teaching is important, but you're still too young to determine that."

"Yes, ma'am," Tiki and Ronde whispered softly.

Their mother never raised her voice once, but she still got her point across loud and clear. "I don't *ever* want to get another report like I got tonight, understand?"

"Yes, Ma."

"If riding the bench in football means you won't be distracted in class, maybe that's the way it's supposed to be. Maybe that's why they don't let most seventh graders start—did you ever think of that?"

Tiki hadn't, he had to admit.

"Now I realize football's important to you boys, but remember, your classes come first."

"Yes, Ma," the boys both said.

"I know if you pay attention in class, you boys will do just fine. You're smart kids, always were. But when you know the answers, you've got to raise your hands. You need to speak up."

"Yes, ma'am," Tiki and Ronde said again, although they weren't happy about it. Not a bit.

"And from now on, I want you boys to do your homework *together*. Just because you don't have the same classes, it doesn't mean you can't help each other. Tiki, you're good in English and history. Ronde, you're good at math and science. If your brother has a hard time with a subject, you help him—and I don't mean do his homework for him, understand?"

"Yes, ma'am."

"You'll both get stronger if you work as a team," she said. "In class, and in football, too."

Funny, thought Tiki. She sounded just like Matt Clayton—he'd said almost the same thing. But how could you work as a team if your job was just to warm the bench?

"Look at me and Mrs. Pendergast," Mrs. Barber said. "We're a team. She's got the passion and the drive, and she's not afraid to knock on strangers' doors. And I guess I've got a way with words. But we *all* have our weak spots, boys. That's why it's good to be part of a team."

"Ma, the way you raised your hand and stood right up there at that meeting?" Tiki said. "I could never do that."

"Me neither," Ronde said.

"I know it takes courage to raise your hand and stand up, boys. You think it was easy for me? You think it was easy to ask people at Back to School Night to sign their names on a petition?"

"Ma, you didn't!" Ronde said. "Not at school!"

"Yes, I most certainly did." She held out her clipboard and smiled. "And I couldn't have gotten all those teachers and parents to sign, if I hadn't stood up and spoken out. But I believe this issue is important enough to risk a little embarrassment. And to give it my time and all my effort."

"Wow, Ma!" Tiki said, flipping page after page.

"How many names did you get?" Ronde asked excitedly.

"Over a hundred, just tonight," Mrs. Barber said proudly. "That's what a person can do when they're not afraid to speak out. Now, you boys need to show a little confidence by raising your hands in class, and calling out the answers nice and loud, so everybody can hear you."

Tiki looked at the page . . . all those names!

"Just like me and Mrs. Pendergast," said their mom, "if you two work together as a team, you'll be stronger than you are alone. Next time I see your teachers, I want to hear nothing but good things. Understood?"

"Yes, Ma," Ronde said.

Tiki nodded. "Yes, Ma!"

If his mom and Mrs. Pendergast could do it, so could he and Ronde.

CHAPTER SEVEN
RIDING THE BENCH

THE DAY DAWNED BRIGHT AND CHILLY, WITH THE wind whipping down from the north. The flags on the flagpoles outside the school and on the field were snapping in the stiff breeze.

On the field, the Eagles kept dancing and hopping and rubbing their hands to stay warm. Across the fifty-yard line, the East Side Mountaineers were doing the same.

Ronde was actually shivering in his uniform as the teams got ready for the first game of the new football season.

The coin toss was won by the Eagles, and they chose to kick off. Coach Spangler had told the team captains he wanted the other team to have to deal with the wind first.

Adam kicked off with the wind behind his back, and the ball went straight out of the end zone! The home team Eagles whooped and hollered, exchanging high fives and waving to their excited fans in the stands.

The Mountaineers tried to run the ball straight up the middle on their first two tries, but the Eagles' defensive line stopped it cold.

The Mountaineers' quarterback tried passing on third

and ten, but the wind held the ball up, making it fall way short of the receiver. The wind affected the fourth-down punt, too. That set the Eagles up at midfield for their first possession of the season.

The Eagles' second-team quarterback was an eighth grader named Cody Hansen. Last year, he'd been the backup for Matt Clayton. This season, though—at least until Matt came back—Cody Hansen was *the man*.

Except that he wasn't. He'd really done well in practice, but as the game got started, Ronde could see that Cody was acting like a totally different player. He nearly dropped the ball handing it off on first down. Then, on the next play, he threw a pass that sailed way over the receiver's head.

"Maybe he's nervous," Ronde said to himself. He could understand that—he figured he would be too, in Cody's shoes.

On third down, Cody completely missed the snap from the center! The ball sat on the ground, spinning in place, while linemen from both teams piled up all around it, wrestling each other to get hold of it.

The refs blew their whistles, separated the players, then signaled the bad news—the Mountaineers had recovered the fumble!

"Aw, man!" Ronde and some of the other kids moaned out loud, but one look from Coach Spangler shut them up.

This is a team, his look said. *We stick up for each other—we don't show each other up.*

Still, as he watched from the bench, Ronde couldn't help thinking that Cody Hansen was messing up, big-time. He felt bad for Cody, sure—but man, the kid was getting his *big chance*, and he was stinking up the joint! Why didn't Coach just pull him, and give the third-string quarterback a try?

Because the third-stringer's just a seventh grader, that's why, thought Ronde.

Tiki sat down next to him and saw the look on his twin's face. "Hey, we don't have to like it," he said. "But we do have to listen to what Coach says."

"I know," Ronde said. "It's just hard, that's all."

The Mountaineers were in Eagles' territory now. Their quarterback snapped the ball, dropped back to pass, then let it fly.

As the ball was released, the wind suddenly calmed down for a moment. The ball flew straight and true. Ronde looked downfield and saw that Justin Aiello, the Eagles' left cornerback, had been badly beaten by the receiver he was supposed to be covering.

"Nooo!" Ronde shouted, but it was way too late. The receiver reached out, grabbed the ball, and ran it easily into the end zone!

The extra point was good, and the Mountaineers led the Eagles, 7–0.

"Hey! Hey!" Coach Spangler barked at the disappointed players coming off the field. "It happens sometimes. Don't let it get you down—good teams get behind, but they find a way to come back."

True, thought Ronde, *but not if their quarterback has a stomach full of butterflies.*

On the Eagles' next possession, starting on their own fifteen-yard line, they ran a couple of plays for Jesse Fowle, last season's star running back. He managed a pair of short gains, mostly by going around end, because the Mountaineers defensive line was so humongous it was scary.

Then, on third down, Cody Hansen dropped back to pass. But the Mountaineers were ready for it. They blitzed, and Cody, under pressure, threw up a lob pass that floated for what seemed like forever. It finally came down—right into the arms of a Mountaineer defensive back—a killer interception, right in the Eagles' own red zone!

Luckily, the Eagles' defense held this time, allowing only a chip shot field goal. Still, the score was now 10–0, and it was only the first quarter!

By the time halftime rolled around, things were looking up, at least a little. The Eagles' defense had kept them in the game, holding the Mountaineers scoreless all through the second quarter.

Still, the way the offense was playing, things didn't look too good—especially after Jesse Fowle twisted his ankle late in the first half.

He'd kept playing on it, but he obviously wasn't the

same runner he'd been last season. Ronde remembered seeing him back then, juking and jiving his way to more than one touchdown.

Not this year—not this *game*, anyway.

The score was now 10–6. The only points the Eagles had in the first half were courtesy of Tiki's and Ronde's old pal Adam. Not only could he kick the ball a mile, but it turned out he could put it straight between the uprights, too!

"So far," Ronde muttered, "he's our MVP."

"I know," Tiki agreed. "Unbelievable."

Neither boy would say it out loud, but it was hard having to sit on the bench while their team was getting creamed.

Well, maybe not *creamed*, exactly. But they would have to come from behind in the second half to win.

The Eagles had been behind only three times all of last season, and they'd managed to win one of those games. But then, that had been with Matt Clayton at quarterback and a healthy Jesse Fowle at running back.

"Listen up, team!" Coach Spangler told them in the locker room between halves. "We're going to have the wind with us this quarter, and their D-line is really big—so I want us to change the game plan and go to the passing game, understand?"

Everyone nodded, understanding the real reason—Jesse Fowle couldn't run, and Coach didn't trust his backups.

"Now get out there and let's get this game back!"

With a fierce roar, the team headed for the tunnel that led back onto the field.

"Man, I hope they put *somebody* else in at running back," Tiki muttered softly as the Mountaineers ran the opening kickoff all the way back to midfield—a bad start to the second half. "I don't care who it is, me or John Berra. Just find somebody who can make a play!"

Ronde felt the same way. He just *knew* that if he'd been in there back in the first quarter, the Mountaineers would never have completed that long touchdown pass. He was *much* faster than Justin Aiello, the Eagles' cornerback who'd been beaten on the play. He just knew it.

Ronde was so wrapped up in his thoughts that he wasn't paying attention to the game. But suddenly, there was a commotion out on the field. The refs were signaling that it was Eagles' ball—there must have been a fumble!

Everyone on the Eagles' sideline cheered and whooped it up, and the offense ran back onto the field.

Suddenly, the momentum seemed to have shifted. Cody Hansen, looking much more confident, completed three straight passes to three different receivers—the last one a perfectly thrown bomb down the sideline all the way to the Mountaineers' twenty yard line.

Then, on first down, Cody dropped back to pass.

But he must have seen an opening, because suddenly, he dashed through the middle on a quarterback draw, catching the Mountaineers off guard. Cody made a quick move to his left, dodged the middle linebacker, and dove into the end zone for a touchdown!

Before the visiting Mountaineers knew what had hit them, they found themselves trailing, 13–10.

Ronde and Tiki got more into the game now. If you had to ride the bench, it sure was more fun to do it when your team was winning!

The game settled in now, with both sides' defenses digging in. The two teams' punters took turns kicking the ball back and forth, but the score remained the same. The big question was, which side would crack first under the building pressure?

In the fourth quarter, the Eagles' defense pressured the Mountaineers into making a pair of costly mistakes. First, their running back had the ball stripped from his hands by Eagles' linebacker Ira Gutzel. That led to another Eagles TD, with Cody connecting on a long bomb to wide receiver Curt Schoenig.

"Man," said Ronde under his breath. He wished it had been him on the field, catching that touchdown pass!

The game quickly turned into a rout as the Mountaineers' quarterback threw an interception. Again, Ronde was torn as he watched Jeff Jacobsen, the Eagles' starting safety, run it back for another TD. Another extra point by Adam (the kid never missed!) and the Eagles' lead stood at a commanding 27–10!

With less than two minutes left, and just when Tiki and Ronde had given up hope of ever getting in the game, Coach Ontkos, who handled the offense, called Tiki's name. Tiki grabbed a helmet and trotted over to him, while Ronde watched and listened.

"Just plow right into the line and hold onto the ball," Ontkos told Tiki. "Don't worry about breaking a big play—we've already got enough points. We just don't want to make any mistakes."

Ronde didn't like hearing that. He knew you could never have enough points. But he understood that the coach didn't want Tiki to risk fumbling the ball by trying too hard to get an extra yard or two.

Ronde sat back down and watched as Tiki ran the ball straight into the line, three times in a row. He gained a total of maybe two yards, but forced the Mountaineers to use up their last two time-outs.

After an Eagles punt, Coach Pellugi called Ronde's name.

"Finally!" Ronde muttered angrily. With only a minute left, the game was basically over anyway. But he was still happy to be in the game.

"You're in at cornerback," Pellugi said, patting Ronde on the shoulder. "Give the receiver lots of room—we don't want any TDs connecting."

Ronde played the next two downs, but they didn't throw to his man, so he never got the chance to make a play. Then the final gun sounded, and the game was over.

The Eagles all jumped up and down, cheering their first win of the season. Everyone chest bumped, high-fived, and gave each other crazy handshakes. Then they lined up to shake the Mountaineers' hands.

When they got back to the locker room, Coach Spangler gathered the team together. "Well, that was a pretty sloppy performance," he said, shaking his head as the team members fell silent.

Then a smile played on the coach's face. "But I'll take a win any way we can get it! A *W* is a *W*."

That brought a big cheer from the Eagles. But Tiki and Ronde just stood there watching. Ronde didn't feel part of it, and he knew his brother didn't either.

"We made lots of mistakes today," Coach Spangler said, "and we're gonna work all this week on our Xs and Os, to make sure we don't make the same mistakes again. Because next week we've got the Bears, and they're not gonna give the game away like these guys did. We've gotta play better, or we're gonna go down. Understand?"

Ronde understood, all right. He understood that it didn't matter how well he and Tiki knew the Xs and Os. If they had to sit on the bench the whole time, what difference would it make?

• • •

Later that afternoon the twins decided to take a break from their home football sessions and go bike riding instead. "Let's head all the way up Mill Mountain," Tiki suggested.

Ronde knew it was a tough ride—uphill all the way. But you could see the whole city from up there, and he thought their mountain bikes could handle it. Besides, making it all the way to the top would be a real challenge—and it would be downhill all the way home.

"Yeah, man, let's do it!" he said.

Riding toward Mill Mountain Drive, they passed Jason jogging the other way. He was wearing a Hidden Valley Track T-shirt, and waved to them, smiling.

"Hey!" he said. "Check this out!" He stuck out his chest, so they could see the T-shirt if they hadn't already.

"Yo, man, you're on the track team now?" Tiki asked.

"That's awesome," Ronde said, as the boys all shook hands. "How'd you get on the team so fast?"

"Are you kidding?" Jason said, still smiling. "It was a breeze. Only about fifteen kids showed up. I'm gonna be the new quarter-miler, starting next weekend."

"Quarter mile, huh?" Tiki said thoughtfully. "I'll bet I could beat you in a quarter-mile race."

"Says you," Jason shot back. "If you're so sure, why don't you quit the football team like I did, and join up? It's got to be boring for you guys, sitting on the bench."

"It is," said Ronde.

"Oh, is it ever," said Tiki.

"I mean, don't get me wrong—now that the track team has got me, they're not exactly desperate. But you guys are mad fast, especially at sprints. I'm sure they'd make room for you."

Ronde was about to blow him off, but he could see that Tiki was giving some serious thought to Jason's words.

"Well, I've gotta keep moving," Jason said. "See you at school."

The boys started riding again, going uphill now that they were in the park. They didn't speak much—mostly because it took all their strength to peddle up the slope. But partly, it was because they were thinking about what Jason had said.

He'd looked so . . . so *happy*, Ronde thought. And why not? Jason had always been fast—almost as fast as him and Tiki. He had every chance to become a track star at Hidden Valley—and so did they, if they would only switch sports.

But that would mean giving up on their lifelong dream! How could they do that?

They rode until they reached the top of the mountain. Then they walked over to the giant neon star and put down their kickstands. Leaning over to the guard rail, they stared down over the city of Roanoke, spread out in the valley before them.

"It sure is pretty up here," Tiki said.

"Yeah, man. It is."

"Ronde?"

"Yeah?"

"What do you think? About what Jason said, I mean?"

Ronde shrugged. "I don't know. You?"

"I don't know either . . . but it sure would be nice to get out there and compete every weekend."

"I'll say."

"You think we'll ever get in a football game? Really get to play some, I mean?"

"Not likely," Ronde had to admit. "Not this year, anyway."

"I'm not waiting till a year from now to play," Tiki said, a hint of anger in his voice. "I'm fed up with sitting on the bench while everybody else gets in there."

"How do you think *I* like it?" Ronde said, suddenly angry himself. "You got in the game before I did!"

"Well, then?"

"What, you want us both to just up and quit?"

Tiki tilted his head, but didn't answer.

"I'm not a quitter," said Ronde.

"Hey, me neither," Tiki said quickly. "I'm just saying . . ."

"Yeah, I know—we could be running the hundred-yard dash by next weekend."

"Right!"

"It's tempting," Ronde admitted. "But we would have to quit football."

"We could try out again next season," Tiki suggested.

"We'd have a better chance of making the starting team as eighth graders."

"Not if we don't hang in there and pay our dues *this* year," Ronde argued. "Coaches remember who stays and who quits. If we join the football team next year, we might not be starters until ninth grade! At least if we stay, we might get to start next year."

"I guess you're right."

"You think so?" Ronde asked, not too sure himself.

"Yeah. Let's just sit tight for now and see how things work out."

"Cool."

"But if we keep riding the bench much longer, I'm gonna explode."

Ronde smiled. He knew just how Tiki felt. "No, you won't," he said. "Hey, we've been dreaming this dream all our lives—it's too soon to give up on it, dog."

"Right," Tiki agreed. "So let's just say we'll give it one more week, and then see what's up."

They slapped five on it and got back on their bikes for the long coast down the mountain. From here on in, the ride would be easy.

Ronde only hoped their football careers at Hidden Valley would go the same way—because it sure had been an uphill slog so far!

CHAPTER EIGHT
HANDS UP!

TIKI SAT IN SCIENCE CLASS, LISTENING TO MR. Wheeler talk about different elements and their electrons. Every minute or so, Mr. Wheeler would throw out a question, like "Silver! How many electrons?" It was like he'd thrown a quick square-out pass that nailed the students right in the numbers.

Hands would shoot up, mostly in the front rows. Mr. Wheeler would scan them with his fierce eagle eyes and serious expression, then extend his arm, point a finger at one of the kids, and say, "YOU!"

Then the kid would have to spit out the right answer. If he or she was correct, Mr. Wheeler would pump his fist and go, "Yessss!"

If the kid was wrong, Mr. Wheeler would fake throwing a rolled-up ball of paper at his or her head. The class would giggle with nervous laughter, glad it wasn't them.

Tiki sat glued to his seat. He *wanted* to raise his hand—after all, he'd promised his mom he would—but he was terrified of actually *doing* it!

Ronde had helped him a lot last night, going over the

periodic table with him until the electron numbers were burned into Tiki's brain.

He *knew* he had the right answers. But somehow, he still wasn't sure enough to risk being wrong. Not in Mr. Wheeler's class, anyway.

It wasn't that it hurt so much getting hit with a rolled-up ball of paper. It didn't—not for more than a second, anyway. It was the *embarrassment* that hurt. All those kids laughing at you . . .

Finally, toward the end of the period, Tiki managed to work up his courage. Remembering his mom's words about standing up and speaking out, he forced himself to lift his arm when Mr. Wheeler said, "Krypton—how many?"

Tiki had to prop his right hand up with his left, to keep it from shaking.

Mr. Wheeler noticed the new hand right away. "YOU!" he said, turning and pointing straight at Tiki. His angry eyes burned through Tiki like a laser.

Tiki stood up, opened his mouth to answer—and froze. For a short, dreadful moment, he actually *forgot the question*!

But then he took a deep breath, and thank goodness, it came back to him.

"Well?" Mr. Wheeler demanded.

"Ei-eight," said Tiki, in a voice not much louder than a whisper.

"What?" Mr. Wheeler said, cupping a hand to his ear.

"Eight," Tiki said again, louder this time.

"I can't hear you!" Mr. Wheeler thundered.

"EIGHT!!" Tiki thundered right back, feeling the blood rushing to his cheeks.

"Eight is correct!" Mr. Wheeler said, pumping his fist. "Yessss!"

Tiki felt a wave of relief flooding through him. He took another deep breath and started to sit back down. "Yessss!" he said under his breath, pumping his own fist in victory.

Mr. Wheeler came over to Tiki's desk. Towering over him, the teacher looked down and said, "Very impressive, Barber. You need to speak up more. Take note, class—Mr. Barber is on it. So . . . no more hiding for him."

The class laughed, but Tiki didn't mind this time. Much to his surprise, raising his hand—and taking a chance on being wrong—had turned out to be a pretty good idea.

His mom had been right after all.

In English class, Ronde's mind kept wandering to what his mom had said. He had been embarrassed the other night, when she came home with bad reports from all his teachers. That had *never* happened before, *ever*—and Ronde was determined that it never happen again.

Their weekend assignment had been writing poems. Once before, in third grade, Ronde had written a poem for class—but it was a really stupid one, and he'd thrown it in the wastebasket rather than show it to his mom.

This time, though, he thought he'd written something pretty decent. That is, he thought so until Ms. Jenkins called on the students to read their poems out loud, in front of the whole class.

After the first few of them got up to read, Ronde found himself squirming in his seat. Their poems were *good*, and Ms. Jenkins said so to each of them.

Would his poem be as good as theirs? Would Ms. Jenkins like it? What if she didn't compliment him after, like she had the others? Maybe she wouldn't get to him before the period ended, Ronde thought hopefully.

But then a little voice in his head—a voice that sounded a lot like his mom's—said, "Be brave and raise your hand, Ronde! Read that poem of yours proudly and don't give in to your fear—conquer it!"

When the next reader was finished, and Ms. Jenkins asked for more volunteers, Ronde bit down hard on his lip, squeezed his eyes shut tight, and stuck his hand up in the air.

"Yes. Ronde Barber, please come up!" Ms. Jenkins said, smiling broadly. She wasn't used to seeing Ronde raise his hand.

But Ronde wasn't smiling. He could feel his stomach going *urgle-gurgle-burble*. He could hear it, too. It was so loud, he was afraid the whole class would hear it and burst out laughing. If they did that, he'd have to just curl up and die, right there in front of everyone.

"My poem is called 'Courage,'" Ronde announced.

He could hear his soft voice trembling. Clearing his throat, he made a real effort to be louder, hoping that would keep it from shaking.

He recited his poem—too fast, but he couldn't help that. He just wanted to get this painful moment over with.

> *"I used to be afraid of heights,*
> *Afraid of the dark, and things that bite,*
> *And strange old ladies who always mumble,*
> *And lions and tigers in the jungle.*
> *Mosquitoes that bite, and bees that sting,*
> *I was afraid of everything!*
> *But then one day I realized*
> *That it might be very wise*
> *To make believe I didn't care—*
> *And what do you know—I wasn't scared!*
> *So if you pretend you're brave and strong,*
> *You will find you can't go wrong.*
> *So what, if your courage isn't real?*
> *It's what you do that matters—not what you feel."*

When Ronde had finished, he looked all around the class. Everyone was staring at him. No one said a word.

Gee . . . was my poem that bad? he wondered.

"That was beautiful, Ronde!" Ms. Jenkins said, putting her hands on his shoulders. "Class, wasn't that a beautiful poem?"

Ronde was really embarrassed, but proud at the same time—and most of all, relieved. Everyone was looking at him, true—but they weren't laughing at him. Not at all!

"Ronde," said Ms. Jenkins, "would you mind if I submitted your poem to the school yearbook committee? They're always looking for good work by seventh graders. I think they might like to put this in this year's edition—would that be all right?"

Ronde was stunned. *My poem—in the school yearbook?* He'd never seen his name in print before.

"S-sure," he said, giving Ms. Jenkins a smile before practically running back to his seat.

Ronde couldn't get over it—he'd written the poem on Back to School Night, after his mom had gotten on him and Tiki. But he'd never realized till he read it out loud—every word in his poem was true!

CHAPTER NINE

Xs AND Os

AFTER SCHOOL, AS THEY CHANGED INTO THEIR Eagles uniforms in the locker room, Ronde told Tiki about reading his poem in front of the class. "You know, I think Mom was right about standing up and speaking out," he said.

"Me too," said Tiki, telling Ronde about what had happened in his science class.

"You know, I've been thinking about it," Ronde said. "Maybe we should stand up and speak out to Coach Spangler."

"Huh?"

"You know—about getting more playing time."

"I don't know . . . ," said Tiki, suddenly feeling nervous.

"Come on, man!" Ronde said. "What do we have to lose? What's he going to do? Bench us?"

Tiki laughed nervously. "You're right, bro. Okay, then. We'll talk to him about it. Tomorrow."

"Tomorrow? Why not *today*?"

Tiki took a deep breath, and blew it out again. "All right," he said. "Today's the day, then."

There was a moment's silence between them. Tiki tried to imagine what it would be like, approaching Coach Spangler about playing time. "Ronde, maybe we should just hang in there and see what happens."

"Come on, don't be a wimp!" Ronde said. "We already agreed on it."

"I know," Tiki said, "but maybe it's not such a good idea."

"Hey, man, no chickening out," Ronde insisted. "Remember, if the worst happens, there's always the track team."

Tiki sure hoped Ronde wasn't wrong about this. Somehow, it seemed to him that there was a *whole lot* to lose. Being a scrub was bad, but getting kicked off the team would be a disaster!

When they were all in uniform, the players gathered in the big lecture room next to the gym. "Okay, team," Coach Spangler addressed them. "Today's practice is all about Xs and Os. We've designed some new plays we want to put in, and today we're gonna try 'em out. It'll be first team on first team, second on second, third on third."

He looked around the big room where all the players had gathered, then turned to the screen. "First slide," he said to Coach Pellugi, who was manning the laptop.

Two lines of letters appeared on the screen. The offense was represented by Xs, the defense by Os. There were eleven of each.

"Okay, we'll call this play 'Notre Dame.' It's a pass play, designed with the wide receivers in mind. Second slide. We line up like this—everybody know which X or O you are?"

Everyone nodded. It wasn't hard to tell—under each X or O were initials indicating which position they stood for: QB for quarterback, WR for wide receiver, RB for running back, and so on.

The new slide showed some of the Xs moving, arrows pointing the way. "The wide receivers are doing a cross pattern here," Coach Spangler said, pointing.

"At ten yards, you make your cut. The fullback blocks out the first defender, while the halfback releases into the flat, about five yards up from the line of scrimmage. He's the third option. Quarterbacks, if neither wideout is free, check off and go to the halfback. If you have to scramble, and nobody's free, just head for the sidelines and get out of bounds—no matter what, don't throw up a pass that could be anybody's ball."

He looked around the room. "Any questions?"

There were a few, after which he went on to the next play—"Alabama"—and the one after that—"Auburn."

"Okay, I think that's enough for one day. Does everybody know their responsibilities for all three plays?"

"Yeah!" all the players shouted.

"Okay! Let's get out there and run 'em until they're smooth as a baby's behind!"

Tiki, Ronde, and all the rest of the players ran out onto the field. "First team, you're up!" shouted Coach Spangler.

While the first team practiced, the second-stringers sat, and the third-stringers did drills. Then the second-stringers took their turn, with the first-stringers doing drills and the third-teamers on the bench.

That was when Tiki and Ronde saw Matt Clayton sitting there. They both went over to join him.

"Hey, guys, how's it going?" he asked, high-fiving them.

"Good," said Tiki. "How about you?"

"I'm getting this stupid cast off on Saturday," Matt said.

"Awesome!" Ronde said.

"I wish it was sooner. I'm gonna have to miss the game that day."

"Hey, no biggie. We'll take care of business for you."

Matt laughed. "You'd better!"

"How soon can you play again?" Ronde asked.

"They said they'll see, once the cast is off. Maybe right away, maybe not for a week or two. But I'd like to see anybody try and stop me from playing!"

Tiki thought about asking Matt whether *he* thought it was a good idea to talk with Coach Spangler about their playing time. But he already knew what Matt would say, because he'd said it before, during tryouts. Maybe Ronde had forgotten his words, but Tiki hadn't:

It's all about the team . . .

"Third team, you're up!" came Coach Spangler's voice.

"Gotta go," Tiki told Matt.

"Catch you later," Ronde said.

"I'll be watching you guys," Matt told them. "Now's your chance to show everyone what you've got—including me."

Exactly what I was thinking, Tiki said to himself.

The offense huddled. Joe Bacino, the third-string quarterback, said, "Notre Dame. On two," meaning the snap was to come on the second "hut."

Tiki got into his stance at halfback. Across the line, Ronde was playing cornerback, defending one of the wide receivers.

"Twenty-five . . . fifteen . . . hut! Hut!"

It all happened in a matter of seconds. The center snapped the ball, and Joe dropped back. Tiki found a hole in the line and jogged casually through it, then turned to face his quarterback. He saw Joe look for his wide receivers. Not finding them open, he looked for Tiki, and fired the ball right into his numbers!

Tiki grabbed it, spun to his right, and sped down-field. He broke one tackle, then another. He spun left, deked sideways, then dodged still another defender and raced for the end zone.

He was going to score!

Wait, no he wasn't—Ronde came out of nowhere. Tiki tried his best spin move, but it was no use—Ronde knew *all* his moves, from years of playing in the street. He made a diving tackle, and Tiki went down.

OOF!

A loud whoop went up from everyone on the sidelines. As the brothers trotted back to the line of scrimmage, everyone was clapping and shouting to them:

"Way to go!"

"Double trouble, yo!"

"Attaway, Barbers!"

Tiki tried not to show any reaction, but he couldn't keep from smiling. Checking with Ronde, he saw the same grin on his brother's face.

But the two didn't dare slap five or celebrate. Both of them knew it was only one play. And unless Coach Spangler agreed to give them more playing time, they'd still be back on the bench that Saturday.

The third-stringers ran the other two plays, "Alabama" and "Auburn." Tiki made another big gain with "Auburn," a running play designed for the halfback.

And guess who brought him down in the backfield? Ronde, *again*.

"Hey, you guys!" Matt Clayton called to them as the third team trotted off the field at the end of practice. "Nice going!"

Tiki and Ronde jogged over to him as he gathered up

his crutches. "I've got a great idea," Matt said. "How'd you guys like to help me work back into shape next week?"

"What do you mean?" Ronde asked.

"I mean, I want to get back on the field as soon as possible," Matt said. "That means I'm gonna have to be throwing every day, and running the new plays so I get familiar with them. You guys have the kind of talent I want to work with."

"Thanks, man!" Tiki said.

"So, is that a yes?" Matt asked.

"Count on it!" Ronde said, and they all high-fived each other.

Tiki and Ronde headed back into the locker room, floating on a cloud. They'd made a big impression in practice, and Matt Clayton had paid them the biggest possible compliment—he wanted them to help him get back into playing shape. On top of that, he'd said they had talent!

Then the twins caught sight of Coach Spangler, sitting alone in a corner, making notes on his clipboard.

And they remembered—their day wasn't over yet.

"It's now or never," Ronde said. "You still game, Tiki? Or are you gonna chicken out?"

Tiki wished he could chicken out. He didn't feel like ruining the good impression they'd made by complaining to the coach like a couple of brats.

But no way was he going to let his brother call him a chicken for the next ten years!

They approached Coach Spangler, standing next to him until he looked up. "Hey, guys," he said. "What's up?"

"Um, Coach," Ronde began. Then he hesitated.

"Yes?"

"Um . . . Tiki wants to ask you something."

"What?" Tiki said. "This was your idea!"

"Shut up!" Ronde hissed.

"Guys! Guys!" Coach Spangler said, holding up his hands. "Somebody tell me what's going on. Please."

Tiki sighed. Obviously, after all Ronde's strutting, he was being a total wimp! "Coach . . . Ronde and I . . . well, our mom always says you should stand up for yourself and speak out when you think something's important."

"I agree," said the coach. "Your mom is a smart lady. What's on your mind?"

"So, um . . . well, we just think . . . we ought to be playing more."

Coach Spangler let out a little laugh, but Tiki could tell he wasn't amused. "Look, kids," he said. "You did very well today. I've seen flashes from both of you. I'm sure you're both gonna be starters for this team someday. And I'm glad you spoke up."

Tiki was starting to feel better about asking, but Coach Spangler wasn't through yet.

"But understand this—I've got seventy kids here, and every one of them wants to play every single down of every single game. Well, it ain't gonna happen. Some kids are gonna play more than others, and the longer they're with the team, the more they're gonna play. Got it?"

"Got it," Tiki said in a small voice.

"Got it," Ronde said, even more quietly.

"You're gonna get your chance to shine," Coach Spangler assured them. "It's gonna happen—probably sooner than you think. In the meantime, though, you've gotta remember—*it's all about the team.* If we win, it's the *team* that wins. If we lose, we all lose together. Now, you want to be starters?"

"Yeah!" Tiki and Ronde said together.

"Then you've gotta earn it, just like everybody else—by being good teammates. And remember, football's a mental game, too. Get your heads in the right place, and the rest will happen naturally in time."

Tiki and Ronde showered and changed back into their street clothes for the ride home on the late bus. They didn't talk much—in fact, they hardly said a word.

Tiki was disappointed. On the other hand, he had to remember all the good stuff that had happened today.

Most of all, he was excited about working out with Matt Clayton. Tiki liked Matt—he was a good guy and a great teammate. No, *more* than a teammate—he'd been the *star* of the team, and was bound to be again, once he came back for real. If Tiki and Ronde became real friends of his, it would be the coolest thing ever!

When they got home, their mom was in the dining room. The whole table was covered with petition forms, all of them full of signatures. Mrs. Barber was mumbling to herself, counting the names. "2,456 . . . 2,457 . . . 2,458 . . ."

"Wow, Ma, *look* at all these!" Ronde said.

"Sssh! 2,459 . . . 2,460! 2,460 signatures! I can hardly believe it."

"That's a lot!" Tiki said. "You did a great job, Ma!"

"Not just me," said Mrs. Barber. "I had a whole team to help me."

"Mom, that sounds like what coach says at practice," Ronde said.

Well, not exactly, thought Tiki. *But pretty close.*

"Did you know that Mrs. Pendergast once had a family of her own?" their mom suddenly said.

"Uh-uh," said Tiki.

"No," said Ronde.

"I didn't know myself, until today. I happened to say something about our campaign—that it was all about keeping my family healthy—meaning you two boys. And she just burst out crying. It turns out her husband and two children were killed in a car crash a few years back."

"What?"

Tiki was shocked, and he could see that Ronde was, too.

"That's right," said Mrs. Barber. "Ever since then, she's devoted herself heart and soul to helping other people and their families."

Tiki felt sorry now that he'd ever called Mrs. Pendergast weird.

"She's somebody to be admired, not feared," said their mom. She let out a sad sigh. "That poor woman. No wonder she talks to herself sometimes. She must be one of the loneliest people on earth."

"Not anymore," Tiki said with a smile. "'Cause she's part of a team!"

"That's right, Tiki. And this team's moving on to victory, don't you worry about that."

"Well, you sure did a good job getting all these signatures," Ronde said.

"Ronde, don't forget—you and your brother are part of this campaign, too. It's for your sakes I got involved in the first place, and I expect you to come to the next council meeting."

"Again?" Ronde and Tiki said together.

"Boys," said their mother, "being a part of a team isn't always fun. Sometimes you've got to show up when you don't feel like it. We need a big showing at this next meeting, and every head counts. You've got heads, don't you?"

Tiki and Ronde laughed. "Sure do," said Tiki.

"Uh-huh," said Ronde.

"Well, then, plan on being there tomorrow night."

"*Tomorrow?* I've got a big test the day after!" Tiki moaned.

"Me too!" Ronde said.

"Well, then," said their mom, smiling, "I guess you'd better get started studying right away."

CHAPTER TEN

THE ROAD TO VICTORY

"HEY HEY—HO HO—THAT NEW FACTORY'S GOT TO GO!!"

Ronde couldn't tell how many protesters there were at the council meeting, but there had to have been a couple hundred, easy. All of them were chanting slogans at the tops of their lungs, drowning out the council president, who was trying to explain why the factory was a good thing for the neighborhood.

Ronde couldn't believe how many people had shown up—all thanks to his mom and Mrs. Pendergast, and the team they'd put together to spread the word.

He looked over at his mom, who was shouting with the others, but smiling too. He was so proud of her!

Even Tiki was chanting—or pretending to. Ronde couldn't hear a sound coming from his mouth, but that was okay. He and Tiki were kind of shy when it came to things like this. Their mom was happy with them just for showing up.

Lots of people in the crowd had signs they were

holding up over their heads. The signs said things like: Keep Our Children Safe, Pollution-Free Zone, and Say No to Toxic Chemicals!

The clerk banged his little wooden hammer, and shouted, "This meeting will come to order!"

But nobody stopped chanting—not until Mrs. Barber raised both her hands in the air for quiet. Then everybody stopped at once.

"Ladies and gentlemen, this council is now in session," said the president. "Tonight we will consider final approval for the factory scheduled to be built on Block fourteen fifty, Map sixteen. Before we take a vote on this, is there anyone present who wishes to say something?"

Everyone in the audience shouted "YES!" and raised their hands.

The president of the council looked stunned. "You *all* want to speak?"

"YES!!" came the reply, echoing off the walls.

"I see. May I just ask for a show of hands—how many of you out there intend to speak *against* this project?"

Everyone in the crowd raised their hands.

The president cleared her throat. "Hmmm. And how many in favor?"

All the hands went down at once.

"I see. Well, in the interest of our long agenda, I'm going to limit comments to twenty minutes."

"NOOOO!!!!" shouted the crowd.

"Please designate someone to speak for you," said the president.

All eyes in the room went to Mrs. Barber. She put her hand to her throat. "Oh, my," she said. "I really think Mrs. Pendergast ought to be the one to—"

"No, no, Geraldine," said Mrs. Pendergast. "It should be you—you're a much better speaker than I am."

"Well . . . all right," said Mrs. Barber.

Coming to the front and speaking into the microphone, she said, "All these people came here tonight because they care about their health, about their families' health, and their children's health. This factory will bring jobs to our neighborhood—we all know that. And jobs are very important—but there are things that are even more important.

"This factory will bring more air pollution, more water pollution. It will poison the vegetables and fruits we grow in our yards and gardens. It will mean more kids with health problems. And just remember, members of the council—we all vote, and we will all remember how you vote tonight!"

The crowd stood up and cheered as Mrs. Barber went back to her seat. The council members all looked at one another. Ronde could see that they were worried.

"All right," said the council president. "It's time for our vote. Mr. Secretary, please call the roll."

A man sitting at the side of the room called their names one by one. Each member said "Yea" for yes, or "Nay" for no. After he was finished, the secretary added up the votes. "The proposal is defeated, six votes to three," he announced.

Another cheer went up from the crowd. Everyone started hugging one another and jumping up and down.

Ronde had to cover his ears, and he saw that Tiki was doing the same thing. The boys made their way to their mom's side, and she threw an arm around each of them.

Ronde was so proud of her! He hugged her right there in front of everybody—even though he thought it was embarrassing to hug your mom in public, where your friends might see you.

Mrs. Pendergast came over and hugged Mrs. Barber too. Then she threw her arms open to Ronde.

Yikes! He realized she was expecting a hug from him, too! Bracing himself, Ronde gave Mrs. Pendergast a hug—and then, so did Tiki.

Sure, she's a little different, Ronde thought. But after all, they had just won a big, fat, huge victory!

Now, if only things would work out as well with the *football team . . .*

It looked like the Hidden Valley Eagles were going to have an even better team this year than the year before. It was only game two, of course. But these were the fearsome Blue Ridge Bears. They had finished second last year, and had beaten the Eagles along the way—one of the Eagles' two defeats all season.

Yet here were the Eagles, leading 27–7, and it wasn't even halftime. And all of this without their star quarterback from last year, Matt Clayton!

Cody Hansen, in his second start, was proving to be a quality quarterback himself. That was a good thing, Ronde thought. Next year, after Matt went on to high school, the team would still be strong at the most important position on the field.

They were looking good at running back, too. Because of Jesse Fowle's twisted ankle, which was still sore from last week and all taped up, Coach Spangler had taken Jesse out once the Eagles built up a big lead. Instead, he'd put in the second-stringer, an eighth grader named John Berra. And Berra was showing that he knew how to run, too.

Tiki was sitting there next to him. *When would the third string get their chance?* Tiki wondered. Ronde was thinking the same thing.

It was just so frustrating, sitting there watching, when they knew in their hearts they could help the team if only they could get in there!

Oh, well, Ronde thought. *Coach rules.* And at least the Eagles had that big lead . . .

Except that in the third quarter, everything started to fall apart.

It was just like what they had done to the Mountaineers the week before. Cody handed off to Berra, but John dropped the ball, and one of the Bears defenders picked it up and ran it in for a TD.

Then, on the kickoff return, Jeff Jacobsen lost the ball on a big hit from one of the Bears. The ball was picked up by another Bears player, who ran it in for a touchdown!

In less than one minute of playing time, the Bears had gotten themselves right back into the game. Now the Eagles' lead was down to six points—27–21.

It was still the third quarter. There was still plenty of time left in the game. Ronde sat there, drumming his fingers on the bench. He was worried that the Bears would score again and win the game.

The important thing for the Eagles was to keep possession of the ball and chew up the clock, so the Bears wouldn't have a chance to come back. To do that, they would have to focus on their running game. And that meant handing the ball to John Berra.

On first down, Berra was stopped for a loss. "Man," Tiki murmured. "He should have cut back!"

"Totally," Ronde agreed.

On second down, Berra was stopped at the line of scrimmage.

"Aw, man," Tiki said, grabbing his head with both hands. "Move the pile!" Turning to Ronde, he said, "I wish they'd put me in just *once*—just *one time*!"

"Me too," Ronde said, thinking of the long pass the Bears had completed for their first touchdown. If he'd been in there, he knew he could have knocked it away—maybe intercepted it, even.

It was third and long now, and Cody Hansen dropped back to pass. The blitz was on, and Cody read it perfectly. He turned quickly, and hit Berra with a perfectly thrown screen pass!

Except that Berra dropped it.

"Oh, man! Catch the ball!" Tiki moaned, trying not to be too loud.

To be fair, the Eagles fans in the bleachers moaned even louder than Tiki. But they didn't have Coach Spangler standing right behind them.

Tiki did.

"*What?*" Coach Spangler challenged him. "What is it, Barber? You got something to say? Say it."

"Uh-uh," Tiki said.

"Uh-uh, what? You don't have anything to say? Or you don't wanna say it?"

"I don't have anything to say," said Tiki.

"Baloney!" Coach Spangler roared. "Say what you mean, son! Speak up, for goodness' sake!"

"I . . . I just didn't think John should've cut to the weak side on second down, that's all."

"Oh, yeah? Maybe *you* would like to try coaching."

"No, sir."

"Because that's a coach's decision." Spangler shook his head in disgust. "You still don't get it, do you?"

"Get what, Coach?" Tiki asked.

Spangler frowned. "I suppose you wanna get in there and take over Berra's job, is that it?"

"No, sir," said Tiki. "I mean, we've got Jesse Fowle sitting over there."

"Fowle's got a bad ankle. Okay, Barber, you wanna get in the game, you're in the game. Next set of downs, you're my running back. Let's see what you've got. Make it happen."

With that, Coach Spangler turned away, walking down the sideline.

Ronde could see that Tiki was blinking back tears. "It's okay, dude," Ronde told him. "Just show the coach what you've got."

Tiki's lip trembled. He bit down on it, sniffed, blew out a breath, and said, "Yeah. That's what I'm gonna do, Ronde. I'm gonna take over this game." They shook hands on it, and Tiki went off to be by himself and gather his thoughts.

When the fourth quarter started, Tiki got his chance. Ronde watched as his twin strapped on his helmet and trotted out onto the field.

Ronde could feel his heart pounding fast, almost as if he were out there himself. "Come on, Tiki!" he yelled at the top of his lungs.

"Come on, Tiki," he repeated in a whisper as the teams lined up for action.

The first play was a handoff. Tiki took it cleanly, and made a beautiful, flashy move to his right, then another to his left, then to his right again. Three Bears defenders went flying head over heels as Tiki broke across the line of scrimmage and headed downfield.

"Yes!" screamed Ronde. "Go, Tiki, go!"

Tiki ran for a good fifteen yards before two Bears tackled him. Tiki refused to go down, dragging both defenders with him for two more yards. Then a third defender knocked him down—so hard that the ball spurted out of Tiki's hands, straight up into the air!

"No! No! No!" Ronde moaned, wincing as the Bears middle linebacker pounced on the ball, recovering the fumble.

"Barber!" Coach Spangler shouted, motioning for Tiki to come off the field.

Just like that, it was over. Tiki trudged back to the bench, slammed his helmet to the ground, and sat down so heavily that the bleachers shook underneath him.

Ronde felt sick to his stomach. Tiki had messed up in front of everybody! He'd blown his big chance—and all because he'd gone and opened his big mouth!

Ronde knew he'd almost gotten caught himself. If Coach Spangler had been standing there one moment sooner, he would have heard Ronde saying the same kinds of things as Tiki.

"Man, I stink!" Tiki grumbled, his lip trembling again. "I

should just quit the team and never play football again!"

"No, you shouldn't," Ronde said, trying to cheer him up. "You're good, man—*really* good. You just tried to get too much yardage on the play. If you'd have gone down as soon as they hit you . . ."

"Shut up, Ronde, okay? Just shut up!"

Ronde was shocked. Tiki *never* talked to him like that—not seriously, anyway. He knew his brother would be sorry later. But still, Tiki's words stung.

The whole rest of the game, the Barber brothers said not one word. Not to each other, and not to anybody else.

Meanwhile, the Bears drove all the way to the Eagle five yard line. Luckily, though—especially for Tiki—the Eagle defense held the Bears to a field goal, and went on to win the game, 27–24.

Ronde didn't know what Tiki was thinking as they got up and headed to the locker room with the rest of the team. But he knew it couldn't be good.

As for himself, there was only one thing he knew for sure: It was way better to sit on the bench and never ask to play, than to get in the game like Tiki had, and then mess up!

Whether to raise his hand in class, or to ask Coach Spangler for playing time, Ronde swore to himself that he'd never stick his neck out—or his hand up—again.

Never ever.

CHAPTER ELEVEN

SPECTATOR SPORTS

". . . MONTANA DROPS BACK TO PASS . . . AND he's got Jerry Rice wide open! Touchdown, Forty-niners!"

"He's awesome!" Ronde said, jumping up from the couch and grabbing another fistful of pretzels.

"Who, Rice?"

"No, dummy—Montana!"

"I think Rice is better."

"Montana's going to the Hall of Fame."

"Rice isn't?"

"Maybe . . ."

"You're nuts," Tiki said, waving his brother away.

It was Sunday afternoon, and the boys were watching the Bears—the *Chicago* Bears—play the San Francisco 49ers on TV. Walter Payton had scored a touchdown in the first quarter on a long run from scrimmage, making Tiki's day.

And now, Ronde's second-favorite quarterback had thrown a game-tying strike.

Ah, Sundays . . . best day of the week, Tiki thought.

Watching the NFL, it was almost possible to forget what a disaster Saturday had been.

Almost. But not quite.

"Do you think I'll ever get another chance to play again?" Tiki asked Ronde when the first half ended.

"Do you think *I'll* ever get a chance to play, *period*?" Ronde replied. "At least you got in the game."

"And I messed up totally," Tiki reminded him.

"Not totally. You made a good run before you fumbled."

"Don't mention that word!"

"Sorry."

Tiki sighed. "I'm tired of sitting around in here. What do you say we go outside and toss it around for a while?"

"And miss the second half?"

"Just for a while, okay? I need to move around, catch some passes—just to prove to myself I can still do it."

"Whatever you say," Ronde said, shaking his head. "But not for *too* long."

They started tossing the ball back and forth. Soon, they were flipping it around behind their backs, and making one-handed shoestring catches, just fooling around, playing for fun.

For fun—that was what had been missing ever since that first day of school, Tiki realized. He'd been too stressed out to have any fun at all—and he was sure it was the same way for Ronde.

"You know what?" Tiki said. "I think we've been stressing too much about the game."

"No lie," Ronde agreed. "I can't remember the last time I felt relaxed on the field."

"We've got to get back to that," Tiki said. "You know, just having fun playing ball, like we always do."

"Like we always *did*, you mean."

"No, man—we can get back to it again," Tiki said.

"I don't know," Ronde said. "Junior high sure makes you feel old."

Tiki sighed. Ronde was right about that, no doubt. He realized that they had both grown up a lot in the past two weeks. Maybe that's what his mom meant when she said middle school would bring growing pains.

If only it had been more *fun*.

"Come on," Ronde said. "That's enough fooling around. The second half must be starting by now."

The boys took the ball inside and settled in for another hour of sitting there, watching other people play football.

And then the phone rang. Tiki was going to just let it ring, figuring it was for their mom anyway.

But Ronde picked it up. "Hello? Oh, hi!" he said, brightening.

Tiki sat up, wondering who it could be.

"Yeah, man—that's cool. Right after school tomorrow? We'll be there. Yeah, no problem. Bye."

He hung up, and flashed Tiki a huge grin. "That was Matt Clayton," he said. "He wants us to work out with him tomorrow after school."

"Yessss!" Tiki said, pumping his fist like Mr. Wheeler.

Suddenly, he felt a surge of energy going through him. Tomorrow, *he'd* be the one out there on the field, actually playing—and with none other than the once and future star of the team, Matt Clayton!

"Hut! Hut-hut!"

Matt pretended to take the snap from center. There was no center there, of course. It was just him, Tiki, and Ronde, and they had the whole empty field to themselves this Monday afternoon, because Coach Spangler had given the team the day off from practice after Saturday's grueling game with the Bears.

Matt dropped back three steps and planted on his newly healed right leg. Then he let the pass fly.

Tiki saw it as a blur, coming straight at his chest. He opened his arms to grab it—and felt it smack off him and bounce away.

"OW! That hurt!"

Matt laughed. "Hey, it's my *leg* that was injured, not my arm."

119

"I'll say," Tiki said, rubbing the sore spot under his jersey. "Man, you can really bring it."

"Let *me* try!" Ronde said, lining up as a receiver. "Come on, Matt, throw me one!"

Matt gripped the ball and threw it. Ronde didn't let it bounce off him, but it knocked him back off his feet, and he landed flat on the field!

"Whoa! That is some serious heat!" he said. "Ow. You're right, man," he told his brother. "It *does* hurt."

"You guys have got to catch it softer," Matt told them.

"What do you mean?" Tiki asked.

"Here. Throw me one." Matt handed the ball to Tiki and jogged down the field, not limping, but not testing his leg either.

Tiki threw it to him as hard as he could. Matt caught it with his arms extended, pulling the ball in until it was cradled against his body. "See? It softens the impact if you catch it like that."

Next, they tried handoffs. "Cradle it!" he reminded Tiki. "Four points of contact, see? That way, it's harder to make you fumble."

After that, they practiced some of the plays Coach Spangler had put in the week before. "Man, I'm rusty," said Matt after overthrowing Ronde on the "Notre Dame" play. "It's really nice of you guys to stay around for me so I can work out."

"No, man, it's fine," Tiki told him.

"No problem. Anytime," Ronde agreed.

The truth was, Tiki thought, this was the most fun they'd had since school had started. Matt Clayton was their first real new friend at Hidden Valley. And *what* a friend—no less than the star quarterback of the football team!

"Now we're gonna put in a special play, just for you and me, Tiki," Matt said. "Sorry, Ronde, but since you're on 'D' . . ."

"That's okay," Ronde said. "It's cool."

"It's a halfback pass option, actually," Matt explained, "so for now, you can play the receiver."

"Excellent!" Ronde said. "I can definitely do that."

"Okay, so I take the snap . . ."

Matt walked them through it. He dropped back and faked a handoff to Tiki, who ran to the right, keeping behind the line of scrimmage. Then Matt pulled to a stop and fired, throwing the ball as far as he could.

It fell ten feet in front of Ronde.

"Okay, we're gonna have to work on my arm strength," Matt said, smiling. "And maybe we'd better change that fly pattern into a buttonhook, Ronde."

"That is such a cool play!" Tiki said. "Too bad we'll never get to try it."

"What do you mean?" Matt asked.

"I mean, by the time I get into a game again, you'll be in high school."

"Don't be so sure," Matt said. "Things happen. The main thing is to be ready when the opportunity knocks."

Tiki nodded. He knew Matt was right. "Hey, when are *you* gonna play in a game?" he asked.

Matt smiled—a big, wide grin. "Saturday," he said. "I'm starting—but don't tell anybody. Coach doesn't want the Rockets to know about it beforehand. He figures maybe it'll freak them out if we surprise them."

"Yeah, baby!" Ronde said. "Sounds good to me."

Suddenly, a loud whistle pierced the air. All three boys turned to see Mr. Wheeler coming toward them, two fingers in his mouth as he whistled again.

"Hey, Clayton!" he shouted. "What happened to those crutches?"

"Going, going, gone!" Matt said, and the two of them high-fived. "You guys know Mr. Wheeler?" he asked Tiki and Ronde.

"I do," Tiki said.

"This little guy's in my class," said Mr. Wheeler, patting Tiki on the back—hard. "He's all right, too—when he stays awake."

Tiki felt the blood rush to his cheeks, and he looked away as the others laughed.

"Hey, Clayton, go long," said Mr. Wheeler. "Let's see if we've still got the chemistry."

Matt gave the ball to him, then ran—fast this time. He didn't seem to be feeling his injury at all, Tiki thought.

Mr. Wheeler waited and waited, until Matt was impossibly far away. Then he threw the ball. It flew straight as an arrow, barely rising, and traveled so far and so fast that Tiki could barely believe his eyes!

Matt reached up with one hand, cradled the ball, and brought it down. All four of them let out a whoop. "Touchdown!" Mr. Wheeler said, raising both hands over his head. "Yessss!"

"Wow, Mr. Wheeler," Tiki said, as Ronde looked on wide-eyed. "You threw that just like a ball of paper!"

"You got that right," he said. He nodded slowly as his smile faded.

Matt was still trotting back toward them when Mr. Wheeler said, "Well, gotta fly." He walked away so quickly that he was out of sight by the time Matt reached them.

"Where'd he run off to?" Matt asked them.

Tiki shrugged. "He didn't say."

"Man, he can throw!" Ronde said. "He could be in the NFL with an arm like that!"

"He almost was," Matt said.

"Huh?" Tiki said.

"Poor Mr. Wheeler," Matt said. "He was a star QB at Clemson before he blew out his knee senior year. The scouts had him pegged as a first-round draft pick, too. I heard the Redskins were drooling over him. He would have broken out for sure."

"Man!" Tiki breathed.

"He's kind of bitter about it," Matt said. "You can imagine how it must have felt." He shook his head sadly. "He helped me a lot my first year here, you know. Made me see what life was all about, in a way. Helped me with my throwing, too, of course."

Now Tiki got it. Maybe that was why Mr. Wheeler sometimes took out his frustrations on the kids in his class. That didn't make it right, of course—but at least now Tiki could understand it. Mr. Wheeler was like Tiki—he wanted to play football more than anything else.

He'd been wrong about Mrs. Pendergast, and about Mr. Wheeler, too. Tiki wondered what else he had been wrong about.

CHAPTER TWELVE
PRESSURE

RONDE WAS REALLY ENJOYING PRACTICE FOR a change. Instead of trying to impress all his coaches and teammates—which never ended up working, it seemed—he was just having fun.

It was sort of like playing on Mews Hill Drive—the results didn't count in the standings. Besides, it was the only chance he and Tiki had to do much playing, because in the games, they were going to be spending most of their time sitting.

So why shouldn't he enjoy practice? Ronde thought.

During today's scrimmage, Coach Spangler had mixed the groups up, to give everybody a new look. He didn't want them getting too comfortable, always practicing with the same people.

Which was how Ronde wound up swatting away a perfectly thrown pass from Matt Clayton to Curt Schoenig.

"Good job, Barber!" he heard Coach Pellugi shout.

Ronde realized that the coach didn't know whether his first name was Tiki or Ronde, but he didn't care. So long as "Barber" equaled "good," that was okay with him.

"Time!" Coach Spangler called suddenly, rushing onto the field and blowing his whistle.

Ronde tried to see what was happening. There was a crowd gathered around somebody lying on the ground. Had one of the guys been hurt?

He rushed over to see, and was shocked to find Jesse Fowle, the team's starting halfback. Jesse was staring into space, grabbing his lower stomach.

"What is it, Jesse?" Coach Spangler asked. "What's wrong?"

"It . . . hurts, Coach," Jesse said, wincing.

"Somebody call an ambulance," Coach Spangler said.

The coaches kept Jesse there, talking to him the whole time, until the ambulance came. Everyone waited quietly, talking in whispers.

"Looks like appendicitis," said one of the paramedics. "He'll be all right once it's taken out."

Coach Spangler made a pained face when he heard that. After the ambulance was gone, he turned and faced the rest of the team. "Well, if it's appendicitis, we're gonna have to make some adjustments, because Fowle may be out for the season. That means we're all gonna have to prepare ourselves. Berra, you'll be taking most of the snaps. And Barber, you'll get your share as well. So let's drop the scrimmage right now, and drill those two into the offense."

In less than fifteen minutes, Tiki's world had changed

completely. Ronde stood there, feeling excited for his brother.

Still, as he watched Tiki taking snap after snap, and knowing his twin would be getting his big opportunity next Saturday, Ronde couldn't help wishing it was happening to him.

Tiki had been on cloud nine all week, floating with happiness and excitement. As sorry as he was about Jesse, he finally had his chance. He wouldn't have the pressure of starting against the North Side Rockets—the strongest team the Eagles would face all season—but he'd get to come in and surprise everybody.

He knew the Rockets would be preparing to face Jesse Fowle, whom they knew from last year. They'd even seen John Berra before, since he'd played in that game, too, as a sub.

But Tiki would be totally new to them—and that could work to his advantage. And when Matt Clayton came off the bench for his first game of the season, they would be in shock—and in trouble.

Still, as Friday rolled around, Tiki could start to feel the pressure mounting inside him. What if he *failed* on Saturday? What if he fumbled the ball away, or didn't block out the blitz, letting Matt get injured again? What if he blew the whole game for his team?

"Barber!"

Tiki snapped to attention, and realized he'd spaced out yet again in Mr. Wheeler's class. But somehow, this time, he hadn't gotten the paper ball fired at his head. Tiki wondered why.

"Yes, Mr. Wheeler?"

"I want you to stay a couple minutes after class today."

"Oooooo . . . ," the whole class murmured, picturing the awful things Mr. Wheeler was going to say to Tiki.

"But I've got to get to practice—"

"I know that," said Mr. Wheeler. "It won't take long—and it's important."

"Yes sir," Tiki said, worrying.

After the bell rang, and all the kids had shuffled out, Mr. Wheeler said, "I know what's been on your mind."

"Huh?"

"I mean, I know why you've been zoning out so much in class this week."

"I haven't been zon—"

"Yes you have, and don't bother to deny it," said Mr. Wheeler. "I mean, you're always something of a space cadet, but this week it's gone into overdrive."

"Sorry, Mr. Wheeler," said Tiki, looking down at his shoes. One of them was unlaced, but he didn't dare tie it now.

"It's because you're going to be playing in the big game tomorrow, isn't it?"

Tiki nodded. "I guess that's right. Like I said, I'm sorry."

"Don't be," said Mr. Wheeler, to Tiki's surprise. "Look, it's a big moment in your life, so you want to make the most of it. That means you've got to keep only positive thoughts in your head. If you start thinking negative thoughts about the game, shift to thinking about something else until you can be positive again. Understand?"

"I . . . I think so," Tiki said.

"Look at what happened to you in this class. At first, you were scared. You were thinking negatively, and you messed up big-time. But then, you got up the courage to raise your hand—and guess what? You were right! And all of a sudden, you had some confidence in yourself, so your work just got better and better."

Mr. Wheeler smiled and nodded slowly. "It can be the same way in football. If you *think* you can do it, you *can.*"

"Hey, it's not about me," Tiki said, smiling back at Mr. Wheeler. "It's all about the team."

Mr. Wheeler clapped him on the back. "You got that right," he said. "Now go out there and get 'em!"

Tiki looked up at the stars—the ones in the sky, and the big neon one at the top of Mill Mountain. He had brought Ronde to their old fort again, to clear their heads and get focused before the big game.

"I'm gonna go out there and *do* it," Tiki said softly.

"That's right," Ronde said. "And I'm gonna yell so loud for you that the other team's gonna go crazy!"

Tiki laughed, and the boys slapped five.

Then slowly Tiki's smile faded. "You really think it's gonna go good?" he asked his brother.

"Go *well*," Ronde corrected him, imitating their mom. Both brothers cracked up.

"Yeah, I think it's gonna go well," Ronde said, smacking Tiki on the back and smiling. "Just don't mess up."

"Mess up? I *never* mess up!"

"Me neither, yo."

"I have never messed up in my whole, entire life!"

"I don't even know the meaning of the words 'mess up'!"

They laughed until they were too tired to laugh anymore. Then they stood up and left for home.

Halfway down the block Tiki turned around for one last look. The old fort stood behind them in the starlight, half hidden in the distance.

Tiki closed his eyes and wished on the stars with all his heart. Then he blew out a deep breath and turned back toward home.

CHAPTER THIRTEEN

THE BIG GAME

RONDE COULD BARELY STAND IT. THE TENSION was just too much. Sitting there on the bench, or pacing back and forth, it didn't matter. Nothing helped.

The Eagles' running game was going nowhere against the North Side Rockets' sturdy line. Berra had had no success on their first two drives, so the third time the Eagles got the ball, Coach Spangler sent Tiki in.

But it didn't do any good. Tiki was managing to hold on to the ball this time—but that was about all. He gained two yards on his first try, one yard on his next. The third time, he was thrown back for a loss of five.

On the next drive, the same thing happened. The Rockets' linemen were just too big and strong—not only for Tiki, but for the Eagles' entire offensive line, including Bryce and Boomer. They sacked Matt Clayton three times in the first quarter. Luckily, Matt got up each time, and was able to keep playing.

Every time Matt went down, Ronde saw Coach Spangler wince, as if his own leg hurt. Ronde could tell Coach was worried about Matt getting hurt again, by the way he barked at the offensive linemen as they came off the field. "Can't you give your quarterback a little protection?" he yelled. "Keep your heads in the game!"

On defense, the Eagles were doing much better. They'd held the Rockets' mighty running game to only twenty-six yards, and allowed only two field goals so far, for a 6–0 lead.

Ronde was too wrapped up in the game to worry about whether he was ever going to get to play in it. He was rooting for Tiki and Matt and the rest of the Eagles with every nerve, muscle, and bone in his body. He jumped up and down in frustration whenever one of the Eagles' receivers dropped a pass.

But worst of all was watching Tiki get creamed every time he carried the ball. The Rockets were piling onto him, and Ronde could almost feel the crush of their combined weight. How was Tiki even able to stand up after that—let alone play?

"Try going outside," Ronde told his twin during one Rockets drive in the middle of the second quarter, when Tiki was resting on the bench. "You know, around the end."

"That's not the play that was called," Tiki explained.

"So what, man?" Ronde said. "Sometimes, when it's not working, you have to make things up as you go. You know—like on the street."

"No, man, it's all about the team, remember?"

"That's what I'm saying, Tiki! You want the team to score some points, or don't you?"

"I don't know," Tiki said, shaking his head. "Things are bad enough. I don't want Coach benching me for going against the play."

"Don't be chicken, dude!" Ronde said. "I'm telling you, they're not ready for you going around end! Just do it—just once!"

"Okay, okay," said Tiki. "Maybe in the second half, if I see an opening."

"Dang!" Ronde muttered, shaking his head and sitting back down. "You are stubborn sometimes!"

Tiki laughed. "That's what Mom always says—about both of us."

Ronde didn't think it was so funny.

Just then, Matt Clayton came up to them. "Hey, Tiki," he said. "How are you holding up?"

"Everything hurts," Tiki said, smiling. "You?"

"I know just what you mean. Listen, next drive, let's go wide. Dump some screen passes to you, maybe run around end."

Tiki looked at Ronde and laughed. "Sounds good," he said.

"Hey, that was my idea!" Ronde said after Matt had walked away.

"I know," Tiki said. "Take it easy, Ronde—two people can have the same idea. It's okay. Just chill, all right?"

"Hey, man—at least you're out there, working your tail off. You think it's easy sitting over here watching?"

"No, man, I know," Tiki said, patting his brother on the arm. "It's tough. Don't worry, though—you'll get in there. Just be patient."

"Ha. Now you sound like Matt."

"It's true, though. Look at me—didn't I get in there?"

"Yeah, you got in," Ronde said. "But you're not *doing* anything!"

"Hey, give me a break—those guys are animals."

"I know it. That's why I say, go around end!"

Tiki sighed. "I've gotta go back in," he said, strapping on his helmet. "It's gonna be our ball."

The Rockets were about to punt. Back to receive the kick was Jeff Jacobsen. The kick was high and wobbly, and Ronde could see that there was no way Jeff would be able to put together much of a runback.

But Jeff wasn't calling for a fair catch. Looking up at the ball, he didn't see the onrushing Rockets headed straight for him.

"Look out!" Ronde screamed, but Jeff couldn't hear him over the roar of the crowd. He caught the ball, juggled it, then got smacked right in the midsection by a flying Rockets rusher!

The ball popped straight up into the air. Another Rockets rusher grabbed it, and sprinted all the way into the end zone. *Touchdown!*

"NOOO!!!" Ronde moaned, along with every other player and coach on the Eagles' sideline.

The score was now Rockets 12, Eagles 0.

But there was even worse news. Jeff Jacobsen was not getting up off the field. He was still lying there, tossing and turning on the ground, and grabbing his stomach with both hands.

Coach Spangler, along with all his assistants and the team trainer, ran out onto the field and surrounded Jeff. Ronde and Tiki could only watch and keep their fingers crossed.

Finally, after about two minutes, the coaches helped the fallen Eagle to his feet. Draping his arms around their shoulders, they helped Jeff off the field—and straight into the visitors' locker room.

Play resumed, and the Rockets converted the extra point. There were still three minutes to go in the first half, but if the lead got any bigger, it was going to be tough to overcome.

Kevin Crandall, one of the team's starting cornerbacks, took the kickoff this time for the Eagles. He was tackled at their own twenty-five yard line.

Matt Clayton came back over to the Barbers. "Come on, Tiki," he said. "Let's get back in this thing."

The offense trotted out onto the field. Matt handed off to Tiki on first down—or did he? Wait, no! He was rolling out to the weak side—and going long! Curt Schoenig caught the pass in perfect stride, and ran it in for a touchdown!

Talk about a quick change in momentum! Ronde couldn't believe it. He was still shouting and jumping up and down when the offense trotted back to the bench. "Way to go, Tiki!" he said, high-fiving his twin.

"Why, what'd I do?" Tiki asked.

"Man, you faked 'em out totally," Ronde said. "Take a little credit!"

"I guess," Tiki said. But Ronde could tell his brother was disappointed it hadn't been him who scored the touchdown.

The extra point was good and the score was now 13–7, Rockets. They took the kickoff from Adam and ran it back to midfield. But during the last two minutes of the half, the Eagles' defense held firm again.

"Okay, we're still in this thing," Coach Spangler shouted as the gun sounded to end the first half. "Let's go, Eagles!" He led them back into the locker room, where all the players drank fluids and tried to get their energy back for the second half.

Ronde didn't need to drink fluids. He didn't need to rest. He was as rested as could be. But he made himself useful, making sure Tiki drank enough and got an ice-cold wet towel to cool off with.

That was when Coach Spangler tapped Ronde on the shoulder. "Barber? I need to talk to you."

"Me?" Ronde asked. "Sure you don't mean Tiki?"

"No, I mean you," said the coach. "C'mere, number five."

He led Ronde over to an empty bench and sat down opposite him. "Listen," he said with a sigh. "We think that Jacobsen has a broken rib."

"What?"

"Yeah, I'm afraid so. We need a new kickoff and punt returner."

"What about Kevin or Berra?" Ronde asked.

The coach shook his head. "Crandall's not used to doing it, and Berra's more of a power rusher. I need a speed demon." He stared right at Ronde. "So . . . what do you think? You ready to be our returner in the second half?"

"Who, me?"

Spangler smiled. "Who am I talking to here? You see anybody else?"

"Yeah, I'm ready, Coach! Put me in!"

Spangler nodded. "All right, you're in. Show me something, Barber—sorry, Ronde. Go out there and show *everybody* what you've got."

"You won't be sorry, Coach!"

Spangler clapped him on the back. "Didn't I tell you you'd get your chance?"

"You did, Coach. I just never thought it would come this fast."

The coach's smile faded, and Ronde knew he was

thinking about his injured player. "Neither did I, Ronde," he said. "Neither did I."

Ronde did some running in place to get himself warmed up. He did some short wind sprints, practicing a few of his patented moves along the way.

But when the big moment came, the kick was so high and deep that all Ronde could do was take a knee. He really wanted to try running it back, but he remembered what had happened to Jeff Jacobsen in the first half—he didn't want to break a rib before he even got started.

"There'll be other chances," he told himself, knowing he'd done the right thing by taking a knee.

On the Eagles' first drive of the second half, Matt faked a handoff and dropped back, pretending to go long. But instead, he dropped a perfect screen pass to Tiki.

The play took the Rockets' defenders completely by surprise. Tiki was all alone in the corner, with just one man to beat. He faked him left, then right, and breezed by his frozen victim into the secondary!

Ronde jumped up and started yelling. "Go, Tiki! Go! All the way!"

Tiki was at the thirty, the thirty-five, the forty, the forty-five, the fifty! The entire Rockets secondary was after him, but Tiki was faster than any of them. It was only the safety, playing deep, who managed to trip Tiki up at the Rockets' fifteen yard line.

The whole Eagles offense mobbed Tiki as he trotted

back to the huddle. Even under his helmet, Ronde could see his brother's big, wide, beaming smile as he high-fived everyone, then ran over to the sideline for a breather.

"Man, you rule!" Ronde said, giving Tiki their best secret handshake. "That was awesome!"

"Felt good," Tiki said, still out of breath. "Felt *really* good."

Out on the field, Matt was calling out the next snap sequence. "Fifteen, forty-three, hut! Hut, hut!" He dropped back, then darted forward, straight past the blitzing linebackers and into the open! He was at the ten, the five . . . *touchdown*!

The whole Eagle bench leapt into the air and let out a huge, triumphant yell.

"Okay, settle down, settle down!" Coach Spangler shouted, motioning them back down. "We don't need any penalties for hot-dogging!"

Adam kicked the extra point right through the uprights, and the Eagles had their first lead of the game—14–13. Then, on the kickoff, Adam really boomed one, knocking the ball right through the end zone.

"Man, that is the longest kick I've ever seen in junior high football!" Ronde heard Coach Pellugi say.

Ronde was proud of their friend, but he had to laugh. Back on Mews Hill Drive, none of them would have ever dreamed that Adam Gunkler would turn into a football star.

And now, after Tiki's big reception and run, there might be two Mews Hill stars on the team! *Too bad I'm not one of them,* Ronde thought with a sigh.

The Rockets weren't through, though—not by a long shot. They had almost won the conference championship last year, before losing to the Eagles in the playoffs. And like the Eagles, they were thinking this was their year to win it all.

The Rockets drove down the field, eating up the clock with run after run. The third quarter ended and the fourth began, and still the Rockets kept coming. They drove to the Eagles' four yard line.

First and goal, with the lead at stake!

On first down they tried throwing it into the end zone—but the receiver dropped the pass! On second down, a holding penalty set them back ten yards. Then a delay of game penalty set them back another five. And finally, a sack by Ira Gutzel set them back another ten yards.

On fourth down, the Rockets sent their field goal unit on. But the kick went wide, and the Eagles took over on their own twenty-nine yard line, still in the lead.

"One more touchdown, and this baby's ours!" Ronde heard Matt say as he took the field.

On first down, Matt looked for his wide receivers, then checked off to Tiki, who had slipped into the flat, and hit him with a short dump pass.

Tiki took the ball and turned to run downfield—but

he was creamed by three Rocket defenders, who all fell on top of him!

The ball must have come loose, because suddenly everyone was diving for it. Ronde watched in horror as one of the Rockets picked the ball up and ran it in for a touchdown! The home crowd cheered, whooping it up as their Rockets celebrated in the end zone.

"Nooo!!" Ronde moaned, along with everyone else on the Eagles' bench.

Then he looked back upfield to see where Tiki was— and he saw that his brother was still flat on his back, lying on the ground!

There was a small circle of players kneeling down at his side, and Coach Spangler was running out there as fast as he could.

Ronde ran, too. He didn't care anymore who won the game. He only cared whether Tiki was okay. He had to push a couple of people aside to get to his brother.

As he kneeled down beside him, Tiki opened his eyes. "Where am I?" he asked.

"You're on the football field, bro," said Ronde, holding Tiki's hand tight. "You got knocked out cold."

"Can you get up?" Coach Spangler asked.

"I . . . I think so," Tiki said. Ronde grabbed one hand, Coach Spangler the other, and they hauled Tiki back to his feet. Everyone clapped—even the Rockets and their fans—appreciating Tiki's toughness.

Ronde draped his brother's arm around his back and helped him off the field. "You sure you're okay?" he kept asking.

"Everything's spinning," Tiki said. "I just need to sit down awhile."

"Take him to the bench and get him some water," Coach Spangler told Ronde. "Coach Pellugi will keep an eye on him. Then you'd better get right back over here. We need you for the kickoff return."

"Kickoff return?" Tiki mumbled. "What happened?"

"You got knocked out," Ronde explained, "and the ball came loose."

"Don't tell me . . ."

"They ran it in for a touchdown, man. Sorry."

"Aw, man! I messed up big-time!"

"No, Tiki—it wasn't your fault, they just creamed you. Nobody could have held on to that one."

"Aw, now we're gonna lose, and it's gonna be all my fault!"

"Barber!" Coach Spangler called.

"Don't worry, bro," Ronde told his twin. "I'm gonna get those points back for us, right now," he said.

Ronde's heart was already beating a mile a minute. He grabbed his helmet, crammed it down onto his head, fastened his chin strap, and ran out to take his position. He lined up at his own ten yard line and waited for the kick.

The score was now Rockets 20, Eagles 14, with only

eight minutes left to play. Ronde knew this might be his only chance to show what he could do—but more important, it was probably his only chance to help his team win the game.

The kick was not a good one—it was high enough, but it was wobbling crazily as it came down. Because it wasn't a long kick, Ronde had to run forward to catch it.

He knew that once he did, he'd be running full speed, right into the onrushing Rockets. If they hit him square, he'd have to hang on to the ball, no matter what!

But first, he had to *catch* it—no easy thing. The ball was spinning end-over-end, and also sideways. Ronde forced all thoughts of getting hit from his mind, and concentrated on the flight of the ball.

OOF!

It hit him right in the numbers. He grabbed it with both hands—cradling it, the way Matt had shown them—and gripped it tightly.

He didn't have time to look and see who was coming at him, and from where. But he knew he had to make a quick move to avoid *whoever* was coming. So he spun clockwise in a full circle to his left, and took off full speed, heading straight downfield.

As he went, he felt a hand reach out and grab for his jersey. It caught his sleeve, but because they were going in opposite directions, Ronde's speed allowed him to break free of the Rocket player's grip.

He saw two more white Rockets jerseys fly by him on either side, even though everything was a blur. Ronde's heart was pounding so hard, he thought it would burst right out of him and flop out onto the field—but he kept running anyway!

The Rockets were converging on him now from every direction. Ronde saw a tiny seam open to his right. He spun again—this time counter-clockwise—heading directly across the field to the right.

All the Rockets, who had been running the opposite way, now had to stop in their tracks and reverse course. While they were doing that, Ronde cut straight downfield again, breaking a tackle by the Rockets' kicker.

He could see the end zone ahead of him now! It seemed so close, and yet so far. From here on in, it was just a foot race between Ronde and one of the Rockets' speediest players. He chased Ronde down the sideline, only a few feet behind him.

Ronde ran for all he was worth. He could barely breathe, and his ears were stopped up by the pounding of his heart so that he couldn't hear the cheering from the Eagles' sideline.

But he knew his teammates were yelling their guts out for him to score. And Ronde was determined to make it all the way to the end zone.

When he was at the five, he could sense that the other boy was making a last lunging leap to try to catch him.

Ronde leapt forward too, stretching the ball out in front of him. He landed in the end zone, and hung on for dear life as the Rockets defender landed on top of him.

Touchdown!

Ronde lay there for a minute, trying to catch his breath. No sooner had he gotten to his feet than he was knocked over again by half a dozen of his joyful teammates, screaming and hollering. The stunned crowd was on their feet, cheering.

Finally, a hand reached out and grabbed Ronde's, hoisting him to his feet again.

"Tiki!"

"Yeah, it's me," said his smiling twin.

"You okay?"

"Yeah, you?"

"Uh-huh. Thanks for picking me up, man," Ronde said.

"No, thank *you* for picking *me* up," Tiki told him. "You did it, bro—you came through big-time!"

The brothers walked off the field together, arms around each other's shoulders.

"I guess you *must* be feeling okay," Ronde said.

"I'm fine, man. Never been better," Tiki said, grinning from ear to ear.

His smile grew even wider when Adam kicked the extra point, giving the Eagles a 21–20 lead.

• • •

The rest of the game was a defensive battle, but the score never changed. The final gun sounded, and the Eagles all let out a victorious roar, hugging each other and jumping up and down.

Ronde sprinted straight into the locker room. He needed a minute by himself, just to make sense of everything that had happened. Had he really scored the winning touchdown in the Eagles' biggest game of the year?

Yes, he had. The lowly third-stringer had come out of nowhere and surprised everybody!

"Ronde?" It was Tiki, standing in the locker room doorway. "Hey, man, everybody's looking for you! Come on, get back out there and get your props!"

"Me?"

Just then, the entire team came pouring through the doorway into the locker room, whooping and hollering at the tops of their lungs.

"Hey, there he is!" Bryce shouted. "Come on, little man—take your lumps!"

He grabbed Tiki, and with Boomer's help, hoisted him onto his shoulders as everybody rubbed his head.

"Ron-de! Ron-de! Ron-de!" they chanted, bouncing Tiki up and down.

"Hey, you guys," Tiki protested. "Ronde's over there! I'm Tiki!"

"Huh?" Bryce let him down, and looked over to where

Ronde was sitting. "Oh, man, these little guys all look alike!"

Everyone laughed. Just then, Coach Spangler came in with the game ball in his hands. "Well, gentlemen," he said. "I guess I know who this goes to."

He handed it to Tiki. "That was one of the best runbacks I've seen in all my years at Hidden Valley. Great going, Barber."

"Thanks, Coach," Tiki said, as everyone laughed. "But you've got the wrong guy."

Now it was Coach Spangler's turn to be embarrassed. "Sorry," he said. "I've got to get your numbers memorized, because otherwise, I'll never be able to tell you two apart."

"That's okay, Coach," Ronde said.

"Just remember," Tiki said, "we're two different people."

"No," Ronde corrected him, putting one arm around his brother and holding the game ball tightly with the other. "We're more than that—we're a team."

CHAPTER FOURTEEN

BETTER DAYS AHEAD

THE CELEBRATION WENT ON FOR ABOUT TEN more minutes. Then they all had to get showered and changed for the bus ride back to Hidden Valley, where their parents were waiting to pick them up.

On the bus, Coach Spangler addressed the assembled troops: "Guys, we can be very proud of what we did today," he said. "That team was the best one we'll face all year. In fact, if you throw the Bears in, we've already beaten our stiffest competition of the season.

"At the beginning of the year, I said I thought we had a chance to go undefeated. I feel even better about that possibility now."

Everyone yelled, cheered, and pounded the walls of the bus with their fists to make even more noise. But just by raising his hand, Coach Spangler turned the noise to silence in seconds.

"But we're not going to get there by letting up," he warned them. "Those other teams may not be as good as the Bears or the Rockets—but any team can beat any other team on any given day. That's the great thing about this game of football, and we're no exception to the rule. We've got to go out there every week and give it our maximum effort, or one day we're gonna lose one of those so-called easy games. And if we do, we'll have only ourselves to blame. Remember, players make plays, but teams win championships."

The silence was deafening, as all the players thought long and hard about what he'd said.

"Now, I've already talked to Jeff and Jesse. They're gonna be okay in a few weeks. But that still means we'll have to win with our subs next week." He smiled, for the first time in his speech. "But I think we've found some good talent today," he said, looking straight at the Barber boys.

The bus erupted into cheers again, and everyone reached out to slap Tiki and Ronde on the back, the head, or the arm. They were so into it, the twins had to duck to avoid getting hurt.

After his speech was over, Coach Spangler came over to them. "Good game, boys," he said. "Both of you. I like the way you play the game, and speed never hurts, either." He sighed. "But I want you to know that once those other guys are ready to come back, you two are back to being subs."

His words took Tiki totally by surprise. He could feel Ronde recoil next to him, too. "But—"

"You played great today, like I said," the coach assured

them. "But I've still gotta be loyal to my veterans. After all, they've put in the time and the hard work. Hey, if it was you, you'd want me to be loyal to you, wouldn't you?"

Tiki and Ronde were silent. They couldn't argue with that.

"But don't worry—now that I know what you guys can do in a big spot, you'll be getting plenty of chances from here on in. And next year?" He laughed, and clapped them both on the back. "Next year, the sky's the limit!"

Those were the words Tiki had longed to hear since he first dreamed of coming to Hidden Valley Junior High. They made him glow with happiness, from the top of his head right down to the tips of his toes. "Thanks, Coach," he said.

"Yeah, thanks!" Ronde echoed.

The bus pulled into the parking lot, and all the kids got out. Mrs. Barber was waiting for Tiki and Ronde with a big smile on her face, and a camera in her hand.

She quickly snapped their picture together, and the flash blinded Tiki for a second. When he could see again, he realized that someone else was there with his mom—Mrs. Pendergast!

"Congratulations, you two!" Mrs. Barber said, beaming. "Congratulations, everybody!"

"Hi, Ma," Tiki said, hugging her. "Hi, Mrs. Pendergast."

"Hi," Ronde said, waving to Mrs. Pendergast before being swept into his mom's embrace. "Ma, you're crushing me," he said, making Tiki laugh.

"Come on, boys," said Mrs. Barber. "We're going out for ice cream—we've all got so much to celebrate!"

At Sweet Treats Ice Cream Parlor, their mom shared some more good news. "The company that wanted to build the factory withdrew their plans!" she said.

"That's great, Ma!" Tiki said.

"Yeah," Ronde agreed. "Now you won't have to do that kind of stuff anymore."

Their mom and Mrs. Pendergast shared a look. "There are always more battles to fight," said Mrs. Pendergast.

"There are?" Tiki said.

"Oh, yes," said their mom. "We've got to do whatever good in the world we can, boys."

"Well, whatever it is, Ma, you can count on us," Tiki said.

"That's right," said Ronde. "We're a team, all of us."

"Oh, I'm so pleased to hear that!" said Mrs. Pendergast. "I think this calls for a Double-Sized Kitchen Sink Sundae— what do you say?"

Tiki said yes, naturally. But he didn't say what he was really thinking—that in spite of being kind of different, Mrs. Pendergast had turned out to be a pretty cool lady.

The sun was just about to set, but Tiki and Ronde were still out on the street, throwing the ball around. It was just the two of them now—Adam and Paco had gone home to eat supper, and Chris and Jason never had time for touch football anymore. Jason had track, and Chris—well, he had debating team, and Model U.N., and Scouts, and a bunch of other stuff.

But the Barber boys didn't mind playing alone. Monday afternoon, they'd be practicing with Matt Clayton again, along with all their new friends on the Eagles.

New friends, Tiki thought. Until now, all his friends were kids he'd known his whole life. And while Tiki knew he never wanted to lose touch with them, or stop being friends with them, he had so much more in common with the guys on the team. It wasn't just them, either—there were some kids in his classes he'd started having lunch with, too.

And of course, there was always his *best* friend—his brother, Ronde. Even though they didn't wear the same clothes or have classes together anymore, they were closer than they'd ever been.

Their mom had been right about that, Tiki thought, as she almost always was about everything.

Man, how lucky were he and Ronde to have a mom like theirs, who stood up and spoke out. She showed them how to be by the way she was herself. . . .

"Yo, wake up!" Ronde said, startling Tiki back to attention. "You'd better go long before I get myself sacked!"

Tiki laughed as he trotted down the street, waiting for the pass to come.

Life was good, he thought, reaching out to haul in the ball.

"Barber makes the grab!" Ronde shouted, doubling as the sportscaster since Chris wasn't around. "Touchdown, Eagles!"

Tiki had to smile. He'd only been at Hidden Valley a month, and look at all he'd learned already.

And to think he'd been nervous about going to junior high! What a start to the year.

FOOTBALL TERMS

blitz: a rush on a passer, usually sending more players than the offense can block.

block: to prevent a player from getting to another player or a specific part of the field.

center: a member of the offensive line who starts a down by passing the ball between his legs to the quarterback.

chip shot: an easy, short field goal.

cornerback: a defensive back defending the wide receiver.

defense: the team attempting to prevent the opposing team from scoring.

defensive back: a player responsible for preventing receivers from catching passes.

down: a complete play, advancing the ball.

end zone: the area where touchdowns are made, located at either end of the field between the goal line and the end line.

fullback: a player in the offensive backfield for blocking and line plunges.

fumble: to lose hold of the ball while it's in play.

halfback: see *running back*.

interception: when the defense prevents the pass of the opposing team, resulting in a change of possession.

line: a demarcation across the field parallel to the end line.

line of scrimmage: an imaginary line that marks the position of the ball at the start of each down.

linebacker: a defensive player who lines up five to seven yards behind the line of scrimmage to make tackles on running plays or defend against short passes.

offense: the team in possession of the ball attempting to score.

possession: control of the ball.

punt: to kick a ball downfield to the opposing team. The ball is dropped from the hands and kicked with the top of the foot before it meets the ground.

quarterback: an offensive player who lines up behind the center, calls signals, and initiates most plays.

running back: an offensive player who lines up in the backfield and whose job it is to run with the ball, block, and catch short passes.

sack: 1. to tackle the quarterback behind the line of scrimmage before he can throw a pass. 2. a kind of defensive back.

safety: 1. when a member of the offense is tackled behind its own goal line, resulting in two points for the defense. 2. a member of the defensive backfield who occupies the deepest position to prevent the other team from scoring.

screen pass: a short pass made to appear as though it will be a long pass in order to fool the defense into rushing forward.

scrimmage: 1. play that begins when the ball is snapped and ends when the ball is dead. 2. when the team practices, playing against itself to experience play as if in a "real game."

KICKOFF!

snap: to put a football into play with a brisk move.

special teams: units usually composed of second- and third-string players on the field for kickoffs, free kicks, field goals, and extra points.

tackle: 1. to stop, seize, or throw down an opposing player in possession of the ball. 2. a strong blocking player on the offensive line, primarily in charge of outside protection. 3. a defensive lineman.

take a knee: an action performed by the quarterback, dropping to one knee after receiving the snap, automatically ending the play. Usually used at the end of a game to run down the clock without putting the ball at risk.

touchdown: being in possession of the ball on, above, or behind an opponent's goal line when it is declared dead, earning a score of six points.

wide receiver: a pass-catching specialist who lines up several yards to the side of the offensive formation. Fast and agile, he or she is often responsible for the biggest plays made by the offensive team.